Blackmail

Amelia Wilde

Chapter One
Will

BILLION-DOLLAR DEALS? COMPLICATED. Hot coffee when I show up? Not complicated. Cream, no sugar. The report I need to review on my desk before the meeting? It should be easy.

Yet here I am, coffee-less. Report-less. And pissed.

My private equity firm, Summit Equity, is in talks to merge with a larger organization. *Merge* is a generous term. They're the Goliath to my David. But David won't mind losing much, not when he gets a cushy executive title and a nine-digit check. And a well-trained secretary, though you'd think I could acquire that for myself.

I can't precisely remember firing my last secretary, but it could have happened. She was the last in a long line of secretaries. Did I fire her? Was it even a woman? I only have fleeting memories of people who are harried and terrified of me and who ultimately fuck things up.

Which means… no one's out there.

My CFO gives me shit about not holding down a secretary for longer than two weeks, but if they can't even get coffee, what's the point? I stand behind my desk, too annoyed to sit.

"Hello," I snap in the direction of my office door. "Coffee. Reports."

A young woman appears in the doorway.

She must have been on her way before I shouted. I'm momentarily ashamed for shouting. For getting so pissed at her over a folder. And coffee, which she's holding.

This isn't my secretary from last week, though.

I barely remember who it was, but I would never have forgotten the full lips and wide eyes on this woman. Her photo could appear in an encyclopedia entry for *beauty,* if an entry like that existed. She has full breasts that don't look demure, even in a white dress shirt buttoned all the way to the top.

"I have your coffee, Mr. Leblanc. One cream, no sugar. Right?" She crosses the room with her head held high, never glancing at the mug in her hands. Her steps are smooth, not one of them jostling the coffee to the rim. In her perfect, cheap little skirt suit, she stops at the edge of the desk, leans in, and places the mug in the center of the waiting coaster. "Is that okay? Oh—here."

She nudges the handle of the mug in the opposite direction.

It's a tiny detail, and one I've never asked anyone to

attend to. In general I've found it pretty fucking pointless to notify my secretaries that I'm left-handed. It should be obvious, given the arrangement of my desk, but all of them have insisted on putting out the coffee like some right-handed asshole is going to pick it up.

All of them except her.

"Who the hell are you?"

"Bristol Anderson." A smile. "From the temp agency."

Christ. We've resorted to temps now. "How long are you here for?"

"Two weeks." She holds up a stack of folders. "These are for your meetings, sorted by schedule."

Two weeks doesn't seem like long enough. I catch the faintest scent of something sweet. And a hint of acidity. Oranges. That's what she smells like, and it makes me want more. I lean closer, but she's looking at me with concern. No more smile. A small notch has formed between dark eyebrows.

"Did something happen, Mr. Leblanc?" Bristol reaches out, and for a dizzying moment I have no idea what the fuck she's thinking. What she's *doing*. What she could possibly be reaching for. And then: "You have a bruise. Here. Are you okay?"

Her fingertips are close enough to feel the air moving ahead of them when I jerk my head away, heart pounding. "None of your business, Ms. Anderson."

She whips her hand back, her cheeks going red. "Are you sure you don't want an ice pack?"

"Did I ask for an ice pack?"

"No." A deep breath, and she lifts her chin. "But you didn't ask for coffee, either. Or the reports. And you seem to want those."

Her eyes are an absurdly breathtaking green. A moment passes, then another.

She wants confirmation on the goddamn coffee.

I pick it up, my soul bristling at the idea that she saw one little bruise and thought I needed *tending*. Maybe she thought she could hold the ice to my face while I worked.

Maybe she thought I would let her do that.

All the bruise means is that I got punched in the face last night.

I'm not explaining to Bristol Anderson that the experience wasn't unexpected. I was prepared for the possibility going in. I wanted a fight, and I got one, though it wouldn't necessarily be sanctioned by the city police.

I glare at her in lieu of saying a word and take an irritated sip.

The coffee is indeed just how I like it. The fact that it's right, that it's how I expected it to be, feels good. It calms the side of me that woke up this morning ready to take another swing at someone. Wanting it, despite how

I spent the better part of yesterday evening.

"Is it right?" Bristol asks.

"It's acceptable." I sit back down at the desk and look into her eyes to emphasize the point.

"It will be ready when you arrive at the office tomorrow," she promises. "I also went ahead and sorted your mail." She moves to drop the folder and the envelopes on the desk, but something else comes down with them, landing as lightly as if a breeze carried it.

Bristol whisks it away, but not before I catch a glimpse. A glossy brochure with a tropical scene on the front. White-sand beach. Palm trees.

Absolutely nothing to do with any of the projects in our pipeline.

Is she making vacation plans? I want to demand more information about that ridiculous piece of paper. It most certainly isn't part of *my* mail, otherwise it would already be sorted into recycling. I don't take vacations. I don't daydream about lying around on the beach.

It's gone through some sleight of hand. Into her pocket, perhaps, or behind her back.

I'm begrudgingly impressed that she came prepared for the next thing I was going to ask her. "What about the invoices that came in?"

"I forwarded them to the finance department."

Fuck, she's good.

Bristol's tone is demure and professional, but her

cheeks are pink. Something about that brochure embarrassed her. She didn't want me to see it, and now I have.

Worse yet, I'm curious. Interested. It's torture, having her in the same room. Bristol Anderson smells too good to fill in as my secretary. She is too gorgeous. And she's trying too hard for a prick like me.

It only drives me back to my base instincts. The ones I learned from my bastard criminal father. The ones I inherited from him.

"Fine."

"I'll be at my desk if you need anything." Her lips part, and if she asks me one more time if I want an ice pack, if I want her to *touch* me, I swear to Satan himself...

Bristol decides against it, and part of me is disappointed. Part of me is a weak, disappointed bastard that she didn't decide to push the issue.

She turns to leave.

"How did you know?" I ask, holding up the coffee.

"Cream, no sugar?" She gives an adorable little grimace. "The temp agency sends me all over. I'm used to jumping in without much guidance."

I raise an eyebrow, waiting.

The words come out in a rush. "I messaged your last assistant on Facebook. He told me how you take your coffee."

"Is that all he told you?"

Her cheeks flush pink. "He had some things to say about you as a... as a boss. I'm used to that, though. No one likes to get fired. I'm sure most of it isn't even true."

"Let's get this straight. Everything he told you? Definitely true. He might have even downplayed it. I'm a bastard of a boss, and it will be a shock if you last the full two weeks."

That takes her aback. Then her chin rises. "We'll see about that."

She waltzes from the room with the bearing of a queen.

I let her go back to her desk, but I watch her until she's out of sight. Watch the fabric of her skirt move against her legs. Watch her hips sway.

Fuck me.

The harder she tries, the more I want to break her down. The more I want to push her. The more I want to see how far she'll go. How far she'll bend.

Because I want to bend her over my desk and fuck her.

It's a problem. I won't be the only one, either. The entire office will want to fuck her. And I have a strict no-office-fucking rule. Company policy doesn't prohibit anyone else from asking her on a date outside of working hours, and I'm sure more than a few of the assholes on my trading floor will try.

In general, emotional attachments with women are bad investments.

They come with an unacceptable level of risk.

I learned that from my mother.

I don't remember the day she left. My brother Emerson told me that she took Sinclair with her to buy bread at the grocery store.

Sinclair came back six months later. Our mother never did.

I flip open the first of the folders Bristol brought and find the report laid out exactly how I want it. Unstapled. Cover memo on the top. The sheets still retain some of the heat from the copier, but the part of me that has no business even speaking to Bristol Anderson thinks it might be her heat on these pages.

I can practically smell her, that delicious citrus scent.

Quiet chatter drifts in the office. The copy machine hums distantly. The elevator *dings*. It's not as quiet as a library, but it's hushed. I like things calm and controlled. By a capable secretary, ideally.

With my coffee and hard copy reports, I can focus on the merger again.

The acquisition, a small voice whispers.

David doesn't mind being swallowed by a rich fucking Goliath, I remind myself grimly.

The offer comes right on the heels of a major success for Summit.

It was the kind of investment that flies under the radar for a couple years. An innovation in billing systems that would sound incredibly boring to most people, but flash doesn't necessarily make the most money. Substance does. When we sold that for big bucks to a Korean conglomerate, everyone in the industry talked about it.

Everyone made offers to invest, but naturally, the bid from Hughes Financial Services was highest. They're the biggest and the best—and they want the company I built.

The merger is good for all of us, but something's been holding me back from signing. I want to look at the final report. Go over the numbers again. And again. They're waiting for me in the hard copy file. I know what they say already. I've memorized every word, every number.

But it's not about the ink on the page. I learned that from Eddie. It's about what isn't there. It's not about the punches someone throws. It's about the pause in between them. The way they telegraph their next moves. The way they show you their weaknesses.

I don't have weaknesses. It's not a statement of pride. It's simply a fact. Any weakness was beaten out of me a long time ago. A rough childhood stripped me of human frailty. I was basically feral when Eddie found me at the warehouse—throwing punch after punch, fighting people two times my weight, getting up when a smarter person would stay down.

He taught me how to fight, but I already knew how to survive.

"Hello?" Bristol's voice, floating in from the vacant secretary's desk in the anteroom of my office, is low and urgent. The panic in her voice is a stark contrast to the smooth corporate flow that was here previously. This call is something serious. "Mia, slow down. I can't understand—what?"

A heavy pause. I'm not even pretending to look at the report.

I can tell this isn't a work call from how frantic she sounds. And the fact that I know no one named Mia. This is personal.

A personal call would be the first strike against this temp, except something tells me that this is a big deal. Something no one should ignore.

Her voice is shaking now. "Are they there right now or did they leave?"

Another pause. I slide my chair a few inches to the right, and I can see her. Bristol is hunched low in front of her desk, her cell phone pressed tight to her ear. What is that on her desk? A small plastic palm tree, looks like, next to a dish of candy. "It's okay. Mia, no. It's okay. I'll be right there. Did Ben lock the door? Oh—okay. Yes, I'll hurry. I love you. Bye."

I slide back into place as she stands up. When Bristol

reaches the door, I look at her over the report. Her face is pale, brow furrowed. She grips her purse with one hand and her phone with the other.

"I'm sorry, Mr. Leblanc. I'm so sorry, but I need to take the rest of the day off."

My heart's beating hard, and it's just from the sound of her voice on that phone call. I'm not going to ask her a damn thing about it. Not a thing. I don't want to care. "Is something wrong?"

"Nothing major." Bristol gives me a bright smile, clearly lying. "Just something I need to take care of. I'll come in early tomorrow to finish my work. I'll have your coffee and reports ready then."

Chapter Two

Bristol

THIS IS BAD.

There's a scale, you know? There's *bad* like getting a C- on your math test, and *bad* like getting a C- on your math test because your dad's landlord decides he's had enough and, oh, it's the middle of the night.

There's *bad* like having an attractive boss and *bad* like sitting tall at your desk, hoping he doesn't notice how hard you're blushing because his face is so gorgeous it makes you feel like the world has taken you in its hands and twirled you around until you lost your breath.

There's *bad* like pissing off your boss at the brand-new temp job that pays well but not well enough to bail out your family, and *bad* like pissing him off because your ten-year-old sister has called to say that someone broke into the apartment and attacked our dad.

I hurry down the cracked courtyard sidewalk with dread in the pit of my stomach. The shitty-apartment surroundings don't help. The sublet in Building C isn't a great situation. Not for any of us. Not for my dad, not for me, and definitely not for my twin siblings, Mia and Ben.

The fact that somebody broke in to beat up my dad isn't exactly a surprise. My sense of dread has nothing to do with shock and everything to do with horrible anticipation.

What has he gotten himself into now?

And how long before it screws the rest of us over?

Really, the question I'm rushing to answer is *how much has it screwed the rest of us over already?*

Take the apartment, for one single example. Subleasing makes our living situation very tenuous. It means we don't have very many rights as renters. It means that if my dad is going to add even more trouble to an apartment complex that already simmers with stress, we might end up without a place to live.

The metal front door squeaks on its hinges. Little pieces of rust fall from the worn kickplate at the bottom. Inside, a sign hangs from a thin chain stretched across the ancient elevator doors. It says *out of order*. The sign was up when we moved in a few months ago. I know it's not going to be fixed. Not anytime soon. I still hold out a faint, silly hope that one day I'll come home and find it whole.

No shortcuts. It's three flights of stairs up to apartment 306. I'm out of breath by the time I get there.

Before I can wrestle my keys out of my purse, the apartment door flies open and my siblings tumble out into the hall. They throw themselves into my arms. Mia tucks herself in first, a half-step ahead of Ben, who wedges himself next to her with an arm thrown over her shoulders. At ten, Ben only has an inch or two on Mia, but he protects her with the energy of someone six feet tall.

"Are you okay?" I rub Ben's back with one hand, holding them close with the other arm. "What happened?"

Mia lets out a breath. "Dad."

"Did he leave?"

"No," Ben answers. He and Mia were born five minutes apart on the same day. They're fraternal twins. She has red hair, and he has dark, but they have matching green eyes. She loves reading, and he loves math, but they're best friends. "Someone came in."

"They knocked on the door," Mia says into my shirt.

"Dad didn't want to open it," Ben continues.

"He stood there for, like, *forever* looking out. But they kept pounding on the door." Mia's voice shakes. "It was so loud. And then the guy said—"

Her voice cuts off, and Ben steels himself. "The guy said he'd shoot out the doorknob if Dad didn't open it."

"So he did?" I ask, forcing my voice to be even. I

want to shatter at the idea of someone shooting a gun into the door while my siblings stand on the other side, but I have to stay calm. I learned that when they were babies. My dad would do something risky, and I'd have to stay calm to protect the twins.

Mia nods.

"Okay." Is there going to be a dead body waiting for me in the apartment? "What did he do?"

"Punched Dad right in the face. He hit his head on the countertop." Ben's trying to be matter-of-fact, but I can hear the wobble in his voice.

"He's not dead." Mia's voice gets even higher. Almost defiant. "Dad fell down, and that guy left. He said something to us, but I don't know what, because…"

"We were too freaked out." Ben's guilty now. "We didn't hear what he said. And then Dad got up. He went into his bedroom and he's been there ever since. I'm sorry. I didn't know what to do."

"That's not your fault." I give them both a squeeze. "I'm just glad you're both safe." Ben won't look at me. "Hey." My brother meets my eyes. Mia peeks up at me, too. "You did the right thing. You called me. I'll take care of it now. Okay?"

"Okay," whispers Mia.

"Let's go inside." Better if we're not standing here on the faded carpet with all the neighbors listening in. They can still listen through the crumbling drywall, but at least we can pretend to have some privacy.

Once the door's locked firmly behind us, I face Mia and Ben. "How was the morning otherwise?"

No school today. Professional development for the teachers. I left them here this morning hoping that they could relax.

They exchange a look. "Fine." Mia bites her lip. "But that guy showed up not too long after you left."

Was he waiting for me to leave? Watching the apartment? I don't like it.

I don't like any of this, but I need to distract them. And I've learned from experience that disasters aren't an excuse from real life. Not when they're so common in the Anderson household. Cooking dinner, doing laundry. Even homework. They still need to be done, even when Dad is blowing everything up.

"Do you have any homework to catch up on?"

Mia says *no* at the same time Ben says *yes*. They both crack a smile when they realize their mistake. I smile back, despite how pissed I am at our dad.

"Go get it done. I'm going to talk to Dad, and then I'll make an early lunch. Deal?"

"Deal." Both of them head to the bedroom they share and close the door. A *squeak* says they've both sat down on their respective twin beds, which take up most of the room.

I go to my own room, which is basically a narrow

closet, and drop my purse on the bed. I *am* going to talk to my dad, but if there's blood—and there's a decent chance of blood—I don't want to get it on my work clothes. The black skirt suit I got on clearance from TJ Maxx goes on a hanger, which goes into its place on a hanging door rack.

Then it's time to survey the damage.

No visible signs of the fight in the living room. Not for the first time, I'm glad we don't have any upstairs neighbors. Building C has six stories in total, but the back corner only goes up three. All that's above us is an HVAC unit and a railing that looks low enough to trip over.

I find Dad in his bedroom, a space barely larger than the twins' room with a half-bath tacked on to it.

He sits in a chair next to a low dresser, which he found left out for free on the curb. It was not easy carrying it up three flights of stairs. His head is tipped back against the wall, and he presses an ice pack to one of his eyes.

No visible blood. I push the door shut behind me and cross to him. It takes all of two steps.

"Let me see."

He opens his uncovered eye. "You don't need to look, Bristol."

Dad sounds tired. Gruff. No surprises there, either. "It's a black eye. That's all."

"I'll be the judge of that. If you broke a bone or damaged your eye—"

"Then what?" He smiles, his tone chiding. Almost bitter. "We'll go to the hospital? I can't pay those people. They're just as likely to arrest me, anyway."

"No one's going to arrest you at the hospital. And if you have to go—"

"I'm not going."

"Let me see your eye." He's not going to lower the ice pack, so I do it for him and wince at the sight of his eye. "Shit, Dad."

A purple bruise curves under his eye socket, darker by the second. I run my fingers lightly over the bone and he hisses.

"Does it hurt that bad?"

"It's not broken. I'm fine." He rearranges the ice pack, hiding the bruise. "It just hurts. He clocked me. I didn't even duck."

"It's probably for the best." He grunts, the sound vaguely disapproving, but he knows I'm right. The guy threatened to shoot the doorknob. He could have shot my dad. "Did he really have a gun?"

Anger swells. There's no doubt in my mind that my dad is not an innocent party. I'm angry on behalf of Mia and Ben, who had to watch it happen. Who could have been *hurt*. I know better than to express that emotion to my dad. It will only get in the way of planning the next steps.

"I don't know. I didn't see it, but that doesn't mean anything. Could have had it in his waistband."

Okay. The real question. The heart of the matter. "What is it this time?"

My dad closes his uncovered eye. "A loan."

"A loan from who?" No bank in the city, probably the country, probably the *world*, will give my dad an actual loan.

"It was more like borrowing," he admits.

Borrowing never means borrowing when it comes to my dad. It means *stealing*. And what he's stolen, he spends. He never has a plan to pay it back. His mouth curves down, and now I know why he's so insistent on keeping that eye closed. He doesn't want to look at me.

"Are you going to pay him back?"

He leans miserably against the wall, his cheeks turning red. "Money's gone. I can't give it back to him. Couldn't, even if I wanted to."

For a good minute, I can't speak. In the end, there's no one else to do it. "You can't keep doing this."

"Bristol…" He takes the ice pack gingerly away from his eye, struggling to keep both of them open. The bruise looks even worse. "Don't you have that fancy job now?"

"Dad."

"Can't you borrow some money?"

"*No*, Dad." I can't keep hot frustration out of my voice. "I'm a temp. It's not the kind of office where they just leave piles of cash lying around."

"Then you have something even better. If it's all money in accounts, all computers..." His eyes glint, hope setting in. "You can sign off on a purchase order."

I stare at him. "A purchase order for what?"

"You're a secretary, right?"

"A *temporary* secretary. The assignment is only for two weeks, and I might not even last that long." Mr. Leblanc certainly hadn't thought so.

"Perfect. God, Bristol, that's perfect." He returns the ice pack to his face, sighing like I've just revealed that we won the lottery. "Just put in a purchase order."

"Again, Dad, for *what*?"

"For anything." He smiles, the gesture half-hidden by the ice pack. "Toilet paper. Coffee beans. Whatever you need in the office. They'll pay it without thinking twice."

"No. Absolutely not."

His visible eye snaps open, and he looks at me with such perfect sincerity that I know it's a con. "He threatened the twins, Bristol."

My stomach drops. Not a con, then. Not a lie. The truth, coming from my dad, is worse. "What did he say, exactly? Mia couldn't tell me. She was too terrified."

"He said he'd come back for them." His hand tightens on the ice pack. "He said that if I didn't pay, he'd come back for them and finish the job."

Chapter Three
Will

THE NEXT MORNING, Bristol doesn't give me a chance to yell for her. She hurries in through my office door five minutes early, a mug of coffee in her hand. There's a tightness around her mouth that doesn't look right.

She's pretty. Beautiful, even. Yesterday she was quick with a smile, and it was real. It went all the way up to those green springtime eyes.

This morning, no smile.

Bristol sets the coffee on my desk, briskly turning the handle in the correct direction.

"Good morning, Mr. Leblanc. I have the latest version of the report you requested from the finance department." The portfolio slides into place near the coffee. "I'll be waiting for the mail. Was there anything you wanted to change on today's schedule?"

Something's up with her. Bristol has another folder

tucked tight to her chest, her fingers gripping the edges so hard the paper bends.

If I had to guess, I'd say this has something to do with that phone call yesterday.

Asking about it would break my life's most important rule, which is to never give a fuck.

But I want to ask her.

I want to know.

"I don't have any changes for the schedule."

Bristol gives me a crisp nod and leaves. Papers shuffle on her desk. A *tap tap tap* as she straightens a stack. A cascade of keystrokes. She's typing like a bat out of hell, like fast, precise data entry will help her outrun what's bothering her.

I spend the next hour wondering what the hell happened yesterday. What made her voice shaky and strained like that? What did she find when she went home?

Where *is* home?

This morning I caved and pulled up her personnel file. We don't have her address because she's technically employed by the temp agency. She's only here for two weeks.

It doesn't *matter* what happened yesterday.

None of my damn business.

But I catch myself staring at the computer screen and listening for the sound of her voice.

More than once.

An email from my oldest brother, Sinclair, arrives in my inbox.

SUBJECT: Back soon

Headed out of town. Back in forty-eight hours. Probably less.

—Sin

I don't need emails to notify me that Sin is leaving town for two days. If my pulse ticks faster, if irritation skates across my rib cage, it's not because I want him to stay. This is a new habit since he came here from LA.

SUBJECT: RE: Back soon

Business or pleasure?

Will

Sin's an investigative journalist who does his best to cover the world's most dangerous locations. When he's not doing that, he's an adrenaline junkie who's gathered a following on social media. His audience is divided between women who want to fuck him and men who want to be him. They all wish they were brave enough for BASE jumping and free-climbing and all the other bullshit Sin posts about.

SUBJECT: RE: RE: Back soon

Little bit of both ;)

—Sin

That probably means he'll be conducting an interview in a war zone and *then* leaping off a tall cliff attached to a set of wings.

SUBJECT: RE: RE: RE: Back soon
Try not to die, asshole.
Will

Sin doesn't send a reply. His plane probably took off already. My mind wanders back to the beautiful temp sitting at her desk, working so industriously to cover up her nerves.

I'm listening for her again when Bristol knocks gently at the door. "Updates from finance."

She's two steps away from the desk when the folder falls out of her hands.

Printed pages go everywhere, fluttering to the floor. I'm out of my seat before I can pretend not to give a fuck. The last page lands as I meet her there on the carpet.

"I'm sorry." Bristol's voice is thin. Breathless. "I had these all in order, and now—"

"It's fine."

Fine, but I'm making a mess of them. Stacking pages together without reading a single word. I reach for the next one at the same time she does.

Our hands brush together.

Bristol's green eyes snap to mine. Wide. Scared. The air in my lungs feels electric. Like she shocked me, damn it, just by a whisper of a touch on my knuckles. My heart's gone out of rhythm.

My brain, too. Because now I can't see anything but her perfect lips. I can't see anything but the pink flush of her cheeks. I can't *do* anything but see her. I'm separated from uncivilized behavior by a heartbeat. By a line as thin as a dollar bill. The things I want to do to her...

Bristol reaches for the paper again.

Let go, a voice in my mind orders. *Let go and get away from her.*

I don't let go. Her fingertips meet mine and she inhales, reaching more deliberately to tug the sheet out of my hand.

"I'm sorry," she whispers.

Sorry for touching me. Her hands fly over the remaining pages. We both stand at the same time, her eyes down at the stack in my hands.

I hand them over, feeling for all the world like I've lost something.

Bristol brushes a lock of hair away from her cheek. "Give me just a minute with these, Mr. Leblanc, and I'll—"

"What's wrong?"

One question. A million broken rules.

No. *One* broken rule, but the biggest one of all. I'm

not supposed to care about Bristol Anderson or any other temp who happens to be sitting in for my secretary. I'm not supposed to care about anything but making more money.

Caring this much about how shaken she is won't pad my bottom line. It won't keep me carefully removed from my worst, most violent instincts.

She blinks, startled, then shakes her head. One of her hands searches out the button on the jacket of her little skirt suit, and she runs her thumb over the edge. "It's really nothing."

"It's clearly something." It's a bastard move, to insist like this.

Her eyes meet mine, wary and gorgeous. I can tell how nervous she is. I can tell how much she wants to tell me her secret, and how scared she is to do it.

"My dad…" That's as far as Bristol gets before she breaks off and looks out the window of my office. New York City is alive outside. Shining skyscrapers. Miles of concrete. Cars for days. The sun reflects off the windows in the building across the street. Her vivid, green gaze comes back to mine. "He means well, but he just won't settle down and work. He's always looking for an angle."

I feel a tug of understanding. Bristol's tone is a familiar one. It's the tone a person uses when their father is a piece of shit, but they don't want to say it in so many words.

"An angle." I straighten up and cross my arms over my chest. "Like a con?"

Bristol nods.

My father is a different variety of bastard. He preferred violence and isolation. My brothers and I might have been better off if he'd been a con man. A *good* one.

"What happened?" I prompt. "Your dad being a con artist isn't the whole story. Why did you have to leave early?"

Bristol hesitates. "Someone came to collect on a debt he owed. It got rough at home."

That's it.

That's the line. This is as far as I'll allow myself to go, because now I have about a million questions. For instance, what the fuck does *rough* mean? Should she have been going back there by herself? Was the asshole still there when she arrived?

Demanding answers is way past the line.

Now I know. I got what I wanted, and now I can go back to work and stop thinking about the temp.

About Bristol.

And yet I find myself frozen in place, looking into her eyes. Her brow furrows, and she worries at the inside of her cheek with her teeth. Does she regret telling me? Is it me who's scaring her, or whoever it was that made things *rough at home*?

Either way, I can't let it go on. She's not at her best.

Early with everything so far today, yes. But she's jittery. It's a recipe for fucking up and losing the company's money.

My money.

"Listen." I have to shut the hell up and get this out of my head. I have to say the magic words to her so she can go back to being a nameless temp and not the woman who's haunting my dreams. "You got a bad break with a dad like that."

Her eyebrows come up. Surprise looks beautiful on her.

"But you can get past it." It feels wrong as hell to be giving advice like this. Wrong, because it reveals too much. Not about her, but about me. About how I had a shitty father, too. One who hit us when he was around. And hitting us was the best-case scenario. I'm fucked up enough to need the lights punched out of me a couple times a month, but Bristol? She's beautiful, smart, competent. She could take over the world if she doesn't let that bastard drag her down. "You do whatever it takes. Understand? You're strong enough."

Strong enough for me.

The thought is barely a whisper. Probably a byproduct of being near someone as fuckable as Bristol.

Her small, tentative smile widens into a real one. "Thank you, Mr. Leblanc. That's nice of you to say." Bristol shakes her head like she's shaking off bad memories. "And you're right. I can handle it."

Bristol leaves with her shoulders relaxed.

I go back to my desk.

What I'm *not* going to do is start caring about Bristol Anderson. My focus will remain on the company, where it's supposed to be.

But I *am* going to keep an eye on her.

I don't like the way she said that things got rough at home. I don't like that it took her out of the office, where I can see her, and back to fuck knows where, with fuck knows who.

If her dad is a shitty con artist who can't pay his own debts, things are bound to get worse. Situations like that only escalate until the prick dies or ends up in jail, like my father.

I type out an email to a guy I know. He's not on the in-house security staff. He's one of my own contacts. Three minutes after I send the email, my desk phone rings.

"Will Leblanc."

"It's Mike. What can I do for you?"

"I need you to look into one of my people." I pause, listening. Bristol's on the phone. From the pattern of her voice, it's a work call. She's occupied. "Bristol Anderson. A temp working at my company."

Filling in until I get another secretary. One who won't leave at the first sign of minor irritation.

"No full background yet, right?"

"No."

The temp agency cleared her to work for me. I don't usually bother with more research into people like Bristol. They're never around for very long. That's the whole point of being a temp. You disappear when you're no longer needed.

"Anything in particular you're looking for?"

"I want to know everything."

"Got it." A pen scratches in the background of the call. "I'll get back to you soon."

Chapter Four
Bristol

I CAN'T DO this.
I have to do this.
It's a dilemma.

I almost broke down in Mr. Leblanc's office earlier. Confessed everything to him. He looked genuinely interested... for a heartbeat. Then that curiosity was gone from his blue eyes.

Not exactly blue. They trend toward green. Breathtaking eyes, actually.

The kind of thing I shouldn't be noticing when it comes to my boss, especially when I'm already on thin ice with him.

He knew something was wrong. I tried to be as put-together as possible this morning. Have everything ready before he asked for it.

Mistake. It made it obvious that I'm freaking out.

Who wouldn't be?

A calendar alert pings on my computer. I rise from my seat, picking up the portfolio I prepared earlier. There's no need to be nervous about giving it to Mr. Leblanc, but my heart pounds.

I tap my knuckles on the doorframe and stride in. Mr. Leblanc stands behind his desk, tapping at something on the keyboard. He stops and straightens up.

"For your three o'clock."

He takes it from my hand, and for a second, both of us are holding on.

Right. I'm the one who has to let go.

"Thank you."

"Do you need anything else?"

"No."

He's back to being his usual terse self, then. I should be relieved about that. If he's not worried about me anymore, his mind is on other things.

I head back to my desk. A minute later, he passes by on the way to his meeting.

Unfair. Really, truly unfair. He looks so good in a suit. The bruise on his cheek from yesterday faded a little. I still wonder where he got it. With as much money as he has, there should be no reason for him to have a bruise. Who would be fighting with him?

When he's out of sight, I turn back to the computer and run my hands over my hair.

I can't do this, but I have to.

Now's the time. Mr. Leblanc will be in a meeting for the next thirty minutes at least. I don't need thirty minutes to put my dad's plan in motion. Ten at most. I can use the other twenty to let my heart stop pounding.

I check to make sure I have everything Mr. Leblanc could possibly need for the afternoon, pat my mini palm tree for good luck, and pop a tropical-flavored Jolly Rancher into my mouth.

Then I click over to the company's purchase order system.

My dad was right about one thing. Mr. Leblanc's company processes a lot of purchase orders. It's a two-floor office space in Manhattan, and it takes more supplies to run the office than you might think. It's not just paper and printer toner. The tiny kitchen alone gets stocked with coffee, tea, sodas, sparkling water, and a small selection of snacks, including gluten-free options.

I feel faintly sick at the sight of the cursor blinking in the memo box.

I hate lies. I hate con men. I hate false things.

But most of all, I hate the consequences of all that bullshit. It's never the con artist who has to pay. Not really. My dad got punched in the face, but it's my siblings who suffer. They're constantly afraid we're going to lose whatever apartment my dad has dragged us to.

I don't blame them. I'm afraid, too. I just don't have the luxury of acting like it.

Pretty ironic that I have to follow one of my dad's cardinal rules. Fake it 'til you make it, right? If I pretend to be confident hard enough, the fear will fade.

That confidence is how I got hired at the temp agency. Honestly, it's perfect. They're an agency with branches all around the country. I applied because I wanted honest work. And when my dad picks up and moves us around again, they can find me a new assignment where we land. The pay here is decent.

Single-person decent. Not rescue-your-family decent.

The twins are ten-year-old kids. They need a lot. Food. Clothes. Things for school.

My dad sure as hell doesn't have the money to pay for those things, much less the rent.

And after the twins went to bed last night, he came clean about how much he really owes to the man with the gun. Fifty. Thousand. Dollars. I couldn't make that much working two jobs at the temp agency. Not even if I worked all day and all night.

The agency also doesn't give advances to bail out your con man father. Mr. Leblanc is probably the only person I've met with enough money to save me, but there's no way I can ask him.

I feel more than a little guilty that it's his voice in my ear right now.

You do whatever it takes. Understand? You're strong enough.

He didn't mean embezzling from his company. I know that. But *whatever it takes* encompasses many things. Out of all of them, this is the best option. It's the only one I can use to guarantee the safety of my siblings.

That's the top priority. Nobody's going to come looking for them. Certainly not a man with a gun.

I'll pay it off. I'll pay it *back*. Of course I will.

My dad swore he'd help. He mentioned a payout, which I dismissed immediately. He promised to get a job.

One deep breath, and I start filling out the purchase form.

Now's the time, because sooner or later, my dad will get angry. He'll lose control. He'll tell the twins that the man is after them, and then neither of them will be able to sleep. They can't function at school on no sleep. They can't run on terror alone.

I don't think my dad would mean to terrorize them. Not necessarily. But he puts himself under this kind of pressure over and over again, and it affects all of us.

I read the instructions embedded in the form carefully. I need it to look real. Not like some stranger walked in off the street and ordered…

What should I order?

My dad said I should order office supplies. A giant order of toilet paper probably won't go unnoticed. So maybe there's something else. Something that even Mr.

Leblanc will be glad to have.

It's coffee beans.

Of course it is.

He only likes a certain kind, imported from Costa Rica, roasted just so. Mr. Leblanc won't tolerate anything else. The old secretary I contacted went on a twenty-minute tirade about the day they ran out of coffee beans. He tried to substitute Starbucks. Knowing it wouldn't go over well, he didn't actually tell Mr. Leblanc about the switch. Which led to quite an upset, apparently.

Mr. Leblanc shook his head in total disbelief.

"If we're *out,* then tell me that," he snapped. "Don't bring me that garbage. Don't expect me to fall for that bullshit." He'd waved the secretary out of his office. "Put in another order. Do it now."

Summit can never have too many of his coffee beans. It's obviously best for everyone if the stock never runs out.

In the end, it's anticlimactic to place the order.

The form guides me through the process. I tap out a description. *Supply restock for Mr. Leblanc's coffee.*

And then, in place of the coffee company's payment information, I enter my own bank account.

My hands tremble over the *submit* button.

I click it and brace for an attack.

An alarm. Some blinking red box on the screen that says, *stop, thief!* A cascade of windows on the screen announcing that I have broken the law and the evidence has been submitted to the NYPD. Officers will be arriving shortly.

Nothing happens.

The order just... goes through.

A small window pops up. Not red. White. It says *transfer complete.*

Holy shit.

With still-trembling hands, I put in another order. A smaller one. This way, coffee actually will be delivered to the office. Everyone will watch it get dropped off. The finance team won't be any the wiser.

And I'm officially a thief.

A criminal.

A con artist, just like my father.

I've handled orders at other companies using similar systems. The money really does pop through the Internet in a matter of seconds. Large bank transfers take fifteen minutes at most.

Shit. What if the bank marks the payment as fraudulent? They might have some system in place to realize that I, Bristol Anderson, would never receive fifty thousand dollars at one time. I grab for my phone, but there's no message there, either.

This moment will forever taste like Tropical Punch. The candy's gone. I must have chewed through it while I committed my crime.

I hold my breath for what seems like a year.

Mr. Leblanc's meeting runs long. At five after five, I switch off my computer, gather my things, and head for the door. I have to get to the bank before it closes at five thirty.

If this con is going to fall apart at the bank, I'm not waiting until tomorrow to find out.

I've got a story in place, too, in case the teller asks about the enormous amount of money. *A death in the family. I was named in the will.* Part of it's true. I did lose my mother, and I do miss her. If I have to, I can summon that sadness.

It was easy to think up the story. Too easy. It makes my cheeks burn with a guilty heat. Was it easy because I'm more like my father than I want to admit? Do I hate liars because it's something I detest about myself?

I'm not doing this for me, though. I'm doing it for the twins.

Or maybe it's an excuse. A flimsy justification for theft. But I don't feel guilty for protecting them. I can't. They're children, and there's nobody else.

All my internal arguments ripple like conflicting currents. The ocean in my travel brochure would never be this unsettled.

The sea has already done the hard work. At the beach in the photo, it's peaceful. That's all I'm trying to do. Buy some peace for my siblings.

The building's elevator cars are all on different floors. I can't breathe, waiting for one of them to arrive. When it does, I have to hold back a cheer.

Silver doors slide open.

And Mr. Leblanc steps out. He narrows his eyes when he sees me standing there. "Ms. Anderson. There you are. I'm glad I caught you."

Oh, no. He means it literally, doesn't he? I'm caught.

My heart stops. I couldn't even pull off embezzlement for an entire afternoon. Two hours. That's how long I lasted.

I picture police and handcuffs and an interrogation light. I picture Mia and Ben, alone. Abandoned. I picture a man with a gun. My muscles lock up tight.

"Yeah?" Very smooth. Very natural. "Yes. I'm still here. Just on my way out."

His expression softens, sharp confusion melting away. "You did well today. I wanted to let you know before you went home for the evening."

"Oh. *Oh*." My knees melt. I could sink right down to the floor and sit there forever. "Oh, thank you. It was no problem. Thank you so much."

Mr. Leblanc shoots me a look. "Have a pleasant evening, Ms. Anderson."

"You too." I sidestep him and bolt into the elevator. "I'll see you tomorrow."

I turn around and find him watching me, suspicious.

There's a flash of hunger in his eyes, I think. Or maybe I just imagine it.

The elevator doors close, and my stomach falls as we descend.

It felt good to hear praise from him. It's not easy to score points with a man like Mr. Leblanc, and I've done it.

I should be proud.

But I haven't won this victory. I've only stolen it.

Chapter Five
Will

IT WOULD BE best for me to go ahead with the merger.

I've been reviewing the reports for weeks on end. The finance department has broken it down for me from every possible angle. They've put together reports on the reports. Spreadsheets. Filings. Everything.

The offer from Hughes Financial Services is airtight. A great offer. A stellar one, even.

For me *and* Summit. It would mean more money and more power. Everything I've always worked for.

But something is holding me back. Woke me up in the middle of the night. I've been at the office since five thirty. It's still quiet out there. Only the overachievers will be in this early.

I get a text message.

Sinclair: *Landed at JFK.*
Will: *That wasn't 48 hours*
Sinclair: *I said it would probably be less. Did you miss*

me?

Will: No.

Did I worry? Yes. Am I going to tell him that? Fuck no.

I have other things to think about. Like Bristol. And this email I've been writing.

The new list of demands hovers on my screen. I've put them in a bulleted list under a corporate-polite note describing how the following items will need to be included in the deal. If they're not, I'll have to withdraw my consideration.

It's a ridiculous list. Absurd. If they want to merge with Summit, they'll have to give me record stock options, control over the company vision, and a superyacht. In other words, it's designed to make them say no. The board will never agree.

They'll call it quits, we'll exchange some genial phone calls about how we all wish it could've worked out, and I'll stay at Summit. We'll all live happily ever after.

Except…

It's not like me to avoid an opportunity like this. Not like me to send a list of demands purpose-built to sidestep my own goals. Not like me to fuck things up.

Here we are.

I hit *send* on the email and watch it leave my outbox.

As soon as it's gone, I feel lighter. Why the hell

would that be the case? Maybe I'm looking for another fight. I just visited the warehouse at the docks a few days ago. The reckless, violent man who hides behind custom suits and strict office policies should be satisfied.

An hour ticks by.

I'm scowling at an empty inbox when my CFO raps on the doorframe. "Am I interrupting?"

Christa Hong is sharp as a tack. I like her because she doesn't miss much.

Between the two of us, Summit hasn't been fucked over once.

"No. Sit." I switch off the computer screen and remind myself, once again, not to think of Bristol Anderson. Not to wonder what the report from my outside man will be.

Christa sits. She purses her lips, managing to look relaxed while she's doing it. As if she's considering which bottle of wine to order at dinner. It rings an alarm bell in my mind.

I've run a company with her for years. Something's wrong.

"You found something in the deal."

"The deal is perfect. Hughes wants us badly enough to give you everything, probably even your damned superyacht. I think your plan of getting them to pull out is going to backfire. They're going to agree."

"Then what's wrong?"

"I found something strange in the accounts."

"Which accounts?"

"That's the thing. It was under the office accounts, which I don't usually review with a fine-tooth comb. Your secretary handles those accounts, which means you sign off on them. But I couldn't sleep last night. I decided to reconcile the books to distract me."

"You could have picked up a novel. Watched a movie."

"My first thought was that it's for escorts. Or drugs. What else could cost that much?"

I don't hire escorts, and I don't do drugs. If I did, I wouldn't pay for them out of company funds. That's what fuckups do. I might be a monster walking around disguised as a civilized person, but I'm not a fuckup. Not when it comes to my business.

"What are you talking about?"

Christa slips her phone from her pocket and taps the screen. "Emailed it to you."

My computer chimes and a notification appears on the screen.

I click on it, and the report expands to fill the monitor.

"The hell is this?" I scroll through, only half-believing what I'm seeing. "Fifty thousand dollars' worth of coffee beans?"

"But then I was like, no, I think Will *would* hire

escorts and buy drugs. But he wouldn't stoop to tax evasion. He'd just pay for them in cash. So I figured something got miscategorized."

"I don't hire escorts," I say absently.

"I'm not judging you."

"I don't."

If I want company, there are other places to find it. If I want entertainment, same thing.

No. The purchase wasn't miscategorized.

Not unless there's a category for embezzlement.

There. I spot it at the end of the form. The bank account numbers aren't for the coffee company in Costa Rica. I know. For one thing, I hunted for the producer of these beans myself after I first tasted the coffee at a small Peruvian restaurant.

For another thing, a code in the right-hand corner of the page identifies which workstation the order was placed from.

The secretary's desk.

Bristol.

It was her.

It makes perfect sense. She was having trouble with her father. Things were *rough at home.*

Fifty-thousand dollars' worth of rough? Maybe.

The right thing to do is to protect the company. Announce to Christa that it was Bristol, and we're going to fire her today and notify the temp agency that she stole fifty thousand dollars from Summit.

I can't do it.

I can't turn my head. Can't even summon the words to my lips.

All I can think about is Bristol. Green eyes. Pale face. The nervous beat of her pulse at her throat.

I'm furious with her. Furious with myself. I don't know which rule I should have broken. The one that says I don't ever give a fuck? The one that says I should never trust a woman like Bristol with anything, much less a desk and access to my accounts?

"Fuck me." At least it sounds genuine. I'm released from my thoughts for long enough to look Christa in the eye. "I placed the order. Didn't want to run out of them. You know I can't think straight unless I've had caffeine. These coffee beans are going to return dividends."

Christa nods, her eyebrows going up. No doubt she remembers the Starbucks incident. That was a particularly bad day. "Well, that explains it. Why is the account number different?"

"It's their wholesale department." My lie is a little too smooth. "Different from retail."

"But... do you have a place to store all of it?"

"Temperature-controlled storage unit down the block."

"Glad I checked with you first." She stands up. "Listen, Leblanc. About that merger. It's going to be good for you. And I'm not just saying that because my small percentage alone will make me rich."

"You're already rich."

"There's always more," she says on her way out.

I'm alone again, listening to the hush of the office. It's a loud silence. My blood heats, then boils. It's stripping the civility from my veins. My clothes feel like a cheap costume. Insufficient to hide the truth underneath. Flimsy, like all the meetings and company policies we use to pretend we've left our base instincts behind.

That *I* use to pretend. All of it chafes.

How dare she?

Bristol Anderson stole fifty thousand dollars from me. From my company. The money already went to her account. It wasn't even attempted theft—she actually did it.

And after I went out of my way to be kind to her. To tell her she could get through that bullshit with her father.

After I wanted her.

I sit back and take a deep breath.

Consider my options.

Calling the police would be easy. Firing her, easier still.

But it wouldn't be as much fun as blackmail.

Catching her red-handed is power. And I'm going to enjoy using it very much.

Chapter Six
Bristol

The elevator at Summit Equity lifts off the ground floor at seven twenty-nine a.m.

That leaves me one minute to get to my desk.

Less than one minute.

Technically, we're supposed to be here by eight thirty, but Mr. Leblanc is always early. That means I need to be here early, too.

And if I know one thing, it's that I can't be even ten seconds late. Not when I owe this company fifty thousand dollars. Not when I owe Mr. Leblanc fifty thousand dollars.

Being late is the perfect way to draw attention to myself. It's bad enough that my desk is twenty feet away from his. I don't need to be sliding home at the last second. Today of all days, I need to be on time.

The elevator doors open and I hustle off, waving to the receptionist on my way past. Her smile is pinched this morning. Something to be worried about? I don't know, and I don't have time to investigate.

Thinking of investigations makes me think of getting caught. It took me forever to fall asleep last night. I dreamed of arrest warrants and cops showing up at my desk. I dreamed of Mr. Leblanc's eyes, but they weren't disappointed. They were heated, almost like he was searching for me.

Hunting for me.

Which is not a thought I can have. Not in the office.

Especially not now.

One of my heels catches on the carpet and my ankle rolls to the side. I right myself before I can fall completely onto the floor, but *ouch*.

I know, I know. I shouldn't rush. Sprinting across the office in high heels is pretty conspicuous.

This morning started out as a struggle. Mia pulled the covers over her head and refused to get out of bed. Ben was up half an hour early, but refused to get ready for school if Mia wasn't doing it.

The whole scene put us at home with our father, which was unbearable.

He was in a fantastic mood. Whistling. Humming. Every time I threw a look at him, he laughed.

"Bristol, don't look so sour. You'll figure it out. It'll be fine."

He's right. I'll figure it out. God knows he's not

going to. I'll figure out how to get the twins to school. I'll figure out how to pay Summit back. I'll figure out how to keep Mr. Leblanc happy, thus keeping my job, until I do.

Finding fifty thousand dollars in less than two weeks isn't impossible. It's new, that's what it is. New and challenging.

Not stressful at all. Just another day in paradise.

I finally had to bribe both Mia and Ben with ten dollars in lunch money *and* walk them to school myself. Five blocks out of the way of my bus route, and then the bus itself was delayed.

As frustrated as I am, I still feel a pang thinking of the twins. They're too old to hold my hand anymore, but both of them seemed reluctant. This morning was a flashback to the first day of kindergarten. They were already late for the first bell, but both of them took a long time to walk away at the school's front doors.

I wish things were stable and law-abiding enough to sign them out for the day and take the train to Central Park. Eat a hot dog on one of the benches and watch people go by.

I *wish*.

Instead, I settled for a tight hug, then pushed them into the front office.

I looked back. Mistake. Mia was watching me through the reinforced glass, the corners of her mouth quivering.

Purse in my desk drawer. Phone tucked inside. Computer on—

"Bristol."

Mr. Leblanc stands in the doorway of his office, his sea-blue eyes darker than they've ever been. The soft, sharp tone of his voice sends a shiver down my spine.

Shouting is more his style.

This is worse.

This is *far* worse.

My smile comes easy, like putting up a shield. "Good morning, Mr. Leblanc."

He doesn't smile back. "My office. Now."

Shit.

He makes no indication he's going to move, so I have to walk past him. *Close.* It only emphasizes that he's tall. Handsome. He has muscles underneath his suit like he does something difficult for exercise, or maybe for torture. It's carved him into a Greek statue of lean muscle and blond hair.

And if that weren't enough, he smells good. Clean. Expensive.

He lives in a nice place and has his clothes sent out. I'm sure of it. I bet it's clean and orderly at his... what? Penthouse? Apartment? I know for sure he doesn't sublease. He *owns.*

It's a distraction from my racing heart.

Mr. Leblanc closes the door behind me. It takes all my willpower to remain facing his desk. I want to turn around and track his every movement. I feel like a wild animal caught in a trap.

His approaching footsteps make all the hairs on the back of my neck stand up.

But I wait, my hands folded in front of me, hoping against hope that I look innocent. That I look like the kind of person he would never call the cops on. Mr. Leblanc—Will, from the business cards at the front of his desk and his email signature, a name I'd never dream of calling him—stalks around behind me.

The air moves with him, almost like we're outside. It stirs a lock of my hair. It feels very much like he touched me himself.

I suppress another shiver.

He faces me from across the desk, eyes hot, like my dream. "Sit down, Ms. Anderson."

I've heard him sound angry. I've heard him sound irritated. This is colder than I could have imagined. Different from before.

I'm not imagining things. I can sense it. He's being snappish like he always is, but there's something bitter and alive about his anger now.

Oh, God. He knows.

No. He doesn't. It's fine.

Of *course* he knows. It was fifty thousand dollars.

He wouldn't miss fifty thousand dollars.

The argument ping-pongs back and forth in my head. Every heartbeat has a different answer.

I sit, my knees weak.

Mr. Leblanc takes his own seat and studies me. I have a powerful instinct to look down, to look away. To hide from him, however I can.

Except there's no hiding now, is there? I'm guilty whether I look at my hands or his eyes.

He lets the silence go on so long that I start to feel deafened by my own heartbeat. It's the guiltiest thing about me, pounding away at my ribs. My own body is trying to give me away.

Not guilty. I'm not guilty. I do my best to believe it. To project the illusion that I believe in my innocence.

My heart ignores this completely. It knows that my innocence is bullshit.

Finally, his eyes narrow. "Do you know why you're here, Ms. Anderson?"

For as long as I can remember, I've been a nervous smiler. It served me well as a kid, except when it didn't. I wish I could get the smile off my face. I wish I could stop.

I can't.

"A quick meeting before we start the day?"

The corner of Mr. Leblanc's mouth lifts. It's not a kind gesture. It's cruel. As if he's only waiting for the perfect moment to attack.

"Better than that. It's time for a performance review."

"A performance review?" I rack my brain for any mention of this in the temp agency paperwork. It's supposed to be my manager at the agency who reviews my performance based on email feedback from whoever oversees me at Summit.

This isn't right.

What am I going to do, argue with him?

Mr. Leblanc leans back in his seat, considering me. "You've been here, what? Two days? That's enough time for me to get a sense of you. Get a sense of what you're capable of."

"Like what?"

It might be best if I fainted. My pulse feels dangerously fast, and my blood feels dangerously thin. Like I don't have enough in my veins for my body to work.

Then what? I'd wake up on the floor of his office. Before that, I'd be unconscious. Vulnerable.

My vision narrows, but I concentrate hard on keeping it together.

I think of the beach. Hot sand and cool water. Waves lapping at the shore. A breeze through palm leaves. Me in a brand-new bathing suit. Me dipping my toes into the shallows, not in jail.

"Like your strengths. And your weaknesses."

The way he says *weaknesses* makes my stomach clench.

"I thought I got your coffee right." I offer weakly. One cream. No sugar. *Not* from Starbucks.

He doesn't laugh at my joke.

He smiles, slow and deadly, the blue in his eyes shaded in green. I have a flash of clarity, as if I'm seeing through an illusion. As if I've been looking through murky water at him, and now I see what he is.

Dangerous.

The hand-tailored jacket slung over the back of his chair doesn't dispel the illusion. It doesn't make him seem less deadly. And it doesn't make me any less afraid.

I blink, hoping he doesn't notice, but I can't unsee it. Will Leblanc doesn't belong in an office. Or the office is what doesn't match. The top-of-the-line furnishings and lemon-fresh scent are a sleight of hand. They're meant to make people think he's not deadly.

This is probably my last chance to run. To get up out of the chair and bolt for the door.

It seems like the right idea. The way to save my life.

I know it wouldn't. He'd catch me, even if I ran. He'd send people after me. I stole fifty thousand dollars from his company, and from the certainty in his eyes, he knows it.

Oh, I could run. And I'd spend the rest of my life wondering when he'd find me.

My chest hurts by the time he speaks. My hands are clenched in my lap.

"The coffee was fine, Ms. Anderson. It tasted delicious. But then, we both know that's not your weakness. That was your strength. It was a distraction. Good, but not good enough. Your father should have taught you better than that. You tried to con the wrong man."

Chapter Seven
Will

BRISTOL ANDERSON STARES at me, wide-eyed, hardly breathing. Her smile sticks on her face, but it's about to die. It's about to falter. There's no way she can keep it up now.

The silence hangs between us.

I don't even know what I planned to do when I finally had her in here. I've had more than an hour to think about it. To be furious. To fantasize.

I imagined calling the cops. I imagined waiting at the front doors of the building and firing her on the sidewalk. I imagined waking up the woman who owns the temp agency at three in the morning and causing chaos.

Those weren't the worst things, though. Those weren't the scenarios that kept me in my office. Those weren't the scenarios that kept my teeth gritted with tension.

I imagined letting Bristol Anderson get away with it.

I imagined knocking on her door with a check for fifty thousand dollars. From my *personal* account, not the business. I imagined pressing it into her hand, no questions asked.

I imagined asking a million questions. I imagined getting all the answers. I imagined listening to her admit to me, in her sweet, pure voice, why she'd stooped to this level.

I imagined hearing the answer and feeling something for her.

I imagined wrapping my arms around her and holding her close.

I imagined telling her that she didn't have to do it, not ever again, because I would fix it. Whatever the problem was, I would fix it.

They were unhinged thoughts. I would never. Not Bristol Anderson. Not anyone.

It made me twice as furious to think about comforting her.

It made me a hundred times as furious that I don't understand.

What would drive a woman like Bristol Anderson to steal? What would possess her to steal from me? Her father? What did he do? What threats did he make? What danger could she possibly be in?

I want to kill whoever it is that made her feel desperate enough to steal. I want to beat the shit out of whoever made her feel so alone that instead of asking for help, she put in a fake purchase order.

It would feel even better to solve a problem for her. Solve it permanently.

That urge is balanced out by several darker ones.

Things I'd like to do to *her*.

It would feel good to stop pretending. It would feel so fucking good to let people understand who I am. *What* I am.

She must see that in my expression, because her eyes get wider. The tension gets thicker. I'm seconds away from vaulting over the desk and—

I don't know what I'll do. I don't know that it's possible to make a conscious plan. I just want my hands on her.

It's like a rubber band stretched across the desk, at its limit, ready to snap. It's the dawning realization that the line between propriety and violence is so incredibly thin. Paper-thin. Money-thin.

Bristol is stock-still. A statue of a gorgeous woman in fear for her life. Her hands are clutched in her lap, trembling.

"We'll start with how you would describe your strengths," I announce, because I'm pissed at her. At me. I want to drag this out. I want to watch her squirm. I want her to feel the way I felt all goddamn night.

"Would you agree that you're skilled in the art of distraction?"

Bristol's cheeks flush. She has to know I'm playing with her. We both know I'm playing with her. But she steels herself and parts her lips.

"No, I—I'm organized." Her voice shakes, but only slightly. "I'm a quick learner. And I learn from my mistakes."

"How quickly?"

"As soon as I know I've done wrong." Bristol's face gets even redder. "I try to fix them right away. As soon as I know how to correct them. The procedures are usually a little different in every job. And I try to know what those are."

What made her do it?

I want to know so much it hurts. I can't even place the pain. It just *hurts*, like being hungry. Or like being punched in the face. The question is on the tip of my tongue. *Why did you do it?*

"Now tell me about your weaknesses."

What about mine? What about the way I was up all night thinking about her? Bristol Anderson is beginning to seem very much like a weakness, which is not something I can have. Not something I would ever allow.

She swallows hard. I can't tell if her eyes are bright with terror or tears.

Maybe it's both.

Part of me would like it to be both. Part of me wants to pull her into my lap and hold her.

Part of me is losing my mind, because I'm not the type to be gentle and comforting. The women I fuck understand that. There's no bullshit. No pretending. And if I were to comfort Bristol, if I were to hold her in my arms and promise her that none of these problems were insurmountable, it wouldn't be pretending.

It would be lying. It would be a con, just like the one she tried to run on me.

I can never be that man. I was fated for violence from the moment of birth. Not softness. Not comfort for a thieving temp.

"Sometimes," Bristol begins. "Sometimes…"

I didn't think it was possible for her face to reach this deep shade of red, but it does. Bristol clasps her hands so tightly her knuckles go white.

She reaches again for that little button at the front of her jacket.

I'd bet anything that Bristol only has two skirt suits. I'd bet anything that she switches them out with a different top each day.

"Your weaknesses," I snap.

And I don't care. I don't care what her weaknesses are. I just want to exploit them. I just want to break her down in front of me so I can pick up the pieces.

"My weaknesses."

The next word out of her mouth should be *you*. That's what her voice sounds like. That's what the energy in the room feels like.

Wrong. Fucking wrong. I'm her boss. Her *temporary* boss.

The way to remove weakness from my life is to banish it. Fire it. Give it a severance package and send it packing. Punch the life out of it and leave it for dead.

There's no room for anything but the business. No room for anything but work. And I've fought for that space. Clawed it out of a soul that wanted fists and blood, not custom suits and stock options.

Bristol's lip quivers, and I see it. She's on the edge. Push any harder and I'll have a sobbing, sweet temp in my office, and there's no telling what I'll do.

"I know what you did, Bristol. I know about the purchase order."

Awareness darkens her eyes. Along with horror. And shame.

Shame looks beautiful on her.

She covers her mouth with her hand, the first fat tears spilling down her cheeks.

I know. I *know*. Someone did this to her. The world is a cruel place. I wasn't lying to her before. She had a bad break with that father of hers. But somehow, I made it to this desk in this building in this business without embezzling money from anyone. Despite the monster inside me, despite the thin veneer of civility that surrounds me, despite every fucking thing.

It hardens my anger and points it at her.

Bristol might be beautiful. She might be young. But she's still a grown woman, and she knew better.

She *knew* better than to steal from me.

She should also know that there will be consequences for those actions. This isn't even everything I want to do to her. I want to spank her ass until it turns pink, then red. I want to rail her until she begs for me to stop, then tell her *no, you can take more.* I want to do every dark and depraved thing I've dreamed about for years.

I've kept it under wraps. Hookups at high-priced bars. A hotel quickie when I'm traveling for work. Even when I play at kink, it's still carefully packaged in socially acceptable paper. Plush handcuffs and a paddle.

None of it reflects what's inside me. The animal that wants to bite Bristol Anderson's skin and leave bruises shaped like teeth. The brute who wants to make her cry. The monster who doesn't want to *play.*

I kept all the options open in my mind last night. I couldn't force myself to choose between them.

Now, looking at her with her dark hair and her full lips and her sweet tits underneath her jacket, I know.

Bristol lets out a choked sob and looks desperately toward the windows. It's a useless gesture. She can't hide from me like that. She can't hide from me at all.

I whisk a tissue from the box on my desk and hand it to her with a sarcastic flourish, like a total asshole. "Take one. Dry your eyes, because we're just getting started."

Bristol accepts it and dabs at her eyes. Her nose.

Then she reaches for the box and pulls the whole thing into her lap.

A tissue box. That's the most comforting thing in the room.

She'll miss it if I deliver the news while she's sobbing into the box of tissues, so I wait. Watch.

Bristol gathers herself.

It happens too fast. It should be harder for her to pull it together. Harder for a sweet temp to draw her shoulders back and blink away the last of her tears. Whatever has happened in her life has taught her to get over things quickly.

One final sniffle and she stands, dropping crumpled tissues into the wastebasket at the side of my desk. The box goes back in its place. Then she looks me in the eye.

"I'm fired. Right? I'll just get my stuff and go."

"Sit down."

Bristol blinks. She worries her lower lip with her teeth. And then, reluctantly, she takes her seat. "I suppose you want to call the police. That's fair. Totally fair."

"You're not fired."

More guarded hope. "I'm not?"

I used to hope, too. I stopped when I discovered it was useless and pursued more tangible things, like money. I doubled down on cold, hard cash again and again. Right up to today. I have so much money that fifty thousand dollars doesn't so much as scratch my finances. It's practically nothing.

"No. You are not fired. What you're going to do, Ms. Anderson, is pay me back."

"I can't. Mr. Leblanc—I can't. I don't have the money. My father—"

"I don't give a fuck about your father. I don't *want* your father." I give her a long look. Take in the tearstains on her cheeks. The full lashes. The dark hair pulled back in a neat bun for the workday. I know what it feels like to be trapped. Which is why I appreciate the fear Bristol is feeling right now.

"What—" Bristol clears her throat. The air around her smells like citrus and fear with an undercurrent of warm desire. There's no mistaking it. I want her to be afraid, of course. I want her to pay for what she did. She'll hate it even more if she wants it, too. "What do you want?"

"I want *you*."

Chapter Eight

Bristol

"No," I whisper.

I know I sound silly. Ridiculous, even. It doesn't feel real. It definitely doesn't feel right.

Maybe it *does* feel right. Maybe I expected something like this. Payment in kind. Maybe a tiny part of me is relieved that he'll accept something other than money.

But most of me is scared to death.

His blue eyes shift colors in the light, changing to a shade like sea glass. Mr. Leblanc's gaze assesses me the way he would any of his daily reports. My breasts. My waist. Back up to my throat.

"Are you a virgin, Ms. Anderson?"

My mouth drops open. No. *No.* I'm never answering that question. Not in the office. Not when it's my boss asking.

"Yes," I admit.

"Be specific." He taps his fingertips on the side of his

leg, impatient. Bored. "Did you let any boys fuck your mouth? Did you offer them your ass instead of your pussy?"

"I—" I can't speak.

"This is a question of value, Ms. Anderson. Answer before I rescind my offer."

"I didn't. I never—I didn't want—" He doesn't care about any of the real reasons. I was busy. I didn't have time to fall in love. I had time for a few crushes at maximum. "I've had a couple of boyfriends, but it never went past—"

An irritated sigh. "Did you suck them off?"

"One of them."

"And did you let them taste you?"

I can't breathe. "No."

Neither one offered. Neither one seemed to register that I might want things, too. There wasn't time for anything real. Not when I had my siblings to worry about.

"What's left will do. We'll start now."

Holy shit. A disbelieving laugh bubbles out of me before I can stop it. "You're not serious."

His expression goes dark. "You stole fifty thousand dollars from my company, Ms. Anderson. You left a paper trail. The evidence couldn't be more cut and dry. The only reason—"

"Mr. Leblanc, I—"

"The *only* reason you're not sitting in a jail cell right now is because I covered for you."

My entire face flames. "You did? But... why? Why would you do that?"

Glittering satisfaction lights his eyes. "Why indeed?"

My heart races.

Because he wanted me. He wanted to fuck me, and now I owe him for more than just the fifty thousand dollars. I owe him for keeping me out of jail.

I have to be out of jail for my siblings. There's no other way they can survive. Not with my dad as unpredictable as he is.

The light in Mr. Leblanc's eyes shifts, his expression changing with it. I'm probably just imagining things. This is already an out-of-body experience. It would make sense that my mind would search for a sense of safety. Of meaning, even.

But I can *see* him.

Behind his cultivated wardrobe and perfect movie-set office, behind his wolfish satisfaction at getting to blackmail me, he's searching. Reaching. As if the cold composure on his face and the hot anger in his eyes are a thin layer between the world and his heart.

A human heart. Maybe even a bruised one.

"What happens if I don't agree?"

He narrows his eyes at my question, and my certainty disappears. I know what he is, and what power he has. I know what danger I'm in.

So it feels wrong to go without a fight. I've always had to stand up for myself. My older brother left for the military before I turned eleven, so it was me against the world.

Me, standing in front of Ben and Mia. My dad, trying to screw things up as badly as he could.

Mr. Leblanc gestures toward his phone. "All it takes is one call."

He'll really do it, then. I let him fuck me any way he wants, or he'll have the police at my desk before I can say *this is against temp agency rules.*

Another vicious smile. "Come here, Ms. Anderson, or go wait at your desk for the boys in blue to get the handcuffs."

The office outside is quiet, but not silent. There are people out there. I could make a scene. I could—I don't know. Scream. Run.

But there's part of me that thinks it might not be so bad to let Mr. Leblanc touch me.

He's tall. He's hot. More than hot. If it weren't for the quickly fading bruise on his cheek, he could have walked out of a men's fashion magazine.

My mouth goes dry.

Quick. Before anyone else comes in.

I go around to the other side of his desk. He points in front of his feet. There's barely enough room for me to fit between his body and the desk. I brush against him as I go, mortified already.

I didn't plan to have sex for the first time in my boss's office.

It's not just my hands shaking now. It's my whole body.

I cling to the fact that he's hot. That he wanted me. That I still have hope. I'm not fired. I'm not arrested.

Not yet.

He brushes his knuckles across the back of my neck, and I jump, my hands flying to my chest.

"Put your hands on the desk."

The result is that I'm bent forward, just slightly, with my palms flat on his desk calendar. Must be fine, because he doesn't comment. He just brushes his knuckles across the same spot again.

This time, I keep it together.

Outwardly, at least. Inwardly, I'm combusting.

He reaches in front of me and strokes one fingertip over the line of my jaw.

His next touch is lower. The front of my neck. One fingertip becomes his whole hand. A gentle squeeze. He doesn't choke me, but I can't breathe. My nipples are painfully hard.

I don't even want to think about what's happening between my thighs. The heat there. The wetness. My body is getting ready for sex. It doesn't care that we're in the office. It doesn't care that he's my boss, and I'm essentially selling my body to pay the debt.

"Keep your hands where they are. Stay still, Ms. Anderson."

Mr. Leblanc waits a beat before he glides his hand down the length of my spine. To my waist. Then lower, to my thighs.

Lower, to the hem of my skirt.

He stops again, and I realize in a hot flush that if I stood up right now, if I ran during one of these pauses, he'd let me go.

He wouldn't follow me.

That makes me want to stay.

He lifts the hem of my skirt, drawing the fabric up and up until it's at my waist.

Mr. Leblanc makes a low sound in his throat, and then his fingertips are in the waistband of my panties.

I suck in a breath before I suffocate, concentrating hard on keeping my hands on the desk.

He pulls my panties down, settling them just below my ass. Then his hand slides between my thighs and tugs.

Wider.

I spread my feet on the floor another few inches.

"Stay."

It's an easy command. Almost like he'd tell a dog to stay. I should be disgusted.

I'm not.

He puts a hand on the curve of my ass. "If someone walked in and saw you right now, what would they think?"

"They'd think you're a pervert," I snap, my hands trembling on the desk calendar.

Mr. Leblanc laughs. "Every man is, darling. Especially with a body as sweet as yours. No. If they saw you with your legs apart and your beautiful ass exposed, they'd know you were my little corporate whore, wouldn't they? Maybe I should use you that way."

He's musing, businesslike, just how he is on the phone with people who want him to invest.

"If someone gets a promotion, you could be the bonus. You'll go into the conference room and service every board member."

"That's horrible," I breathe.

But secretly, awfully, I find the idea hot.

Especially if it was with Mr. Leblanc. Especially if his hand was in my hair. Especially if he made me do it.

"Stay," he says again.

One heartbeat.

Then his hand is between my legs.

I gasp. It's not the harsh touch I was expecting, but it's not exactly gentle. He's possessive about stroking me there. Exploring. Like he's testing out what he bought.

One of my thighs tries to sneak inward and trap his

hand, but he stops me with a single, disapproving noise.

I've become a different person in the last five minutes. A woman who spreads her legs even wider for her boss.

That's not the reason I'm wet. Not the reason I'm soaked. Not the reason I'm having trouble staying still. And it isn't because I don't want him to touch me. It's that I want more contact, and he doesn't give it to me. His fingertips circle my hole.

I *hear* it. That's how wet I am.

"Oh, Ms. Anderson," he scolds. "Are you sure you didn't get caught stealing fifty thousand dollars on purpose?"

I open my mouth to protest, but I don't get the chance. Mr. Leblanc's fingertips meet my clit, and I let out a low moan. "No."

Small circles. Even pressure. "That was a little loud, don't you think? I'm certain you don't want the rest of the office to hear."

I pinch my lips shut.

He knows what he's doing. He's touching me the way I want now. Fingertips moving. Palm over my folds. I find myself arching back for him even while embarrassment eats me alive.

If I die from this, at least I won't owe anyone any money.

But that doesn't happen. I stand there, I *stay*, with

Mr. Leblanc's hand working between my legs. Circling my clit. I'm on the edge. My thighs shake.

This—this is what's wrong.

He could make me come, but he just keeps making those maddening circles. I'm so close. I could do it. I could orgasm in this humiliating position and not make a single sound, I want it that badly.

"You want to come, don't you?" he murmurs.

"*Yes.*" The word struggles past gritted teeth.

"Poor thing."

One more circle, and his hand is gone. He tugs my panties up and lets the waistband snap into place. Flips my skirt down.

I'm frozen with my palms on the desk.

Mr. Leblanc snaps his fingers. "Up."

"You—" You can't be serious. That's what I want to say. You can't leave me this way. Wet and unsatisfied and embarrassed. I have no other clothes to change into. I just have to live like this all day.

A cruel grin says he's done it on purpose. "You have work to do, Ms. Anderson. Go back to your desk."

Chapter Nine
Bristol

Mia stands in the doorway to my bedroom, her arms crossed over her chest. She sticks her chin out. There's a defiant fire in her eyes.

"I don't want to go back, Bristol. It's not fun there. I'm always getting into trouble for nothing."

I meet her eyes in the mirror as I slide the backs onto the second of a pair of cheap pearl studs. Duane Reade, I think. I'm careful to keep my expression nonjudgmental. "Your teacher said you have trouble sitting still in class. That doesn't mean you *are* trouble. And it doesn't mean you can't have fun."

"Yes, it *does* mean that. I can't have any fun." Her eyes slide to the window, and I see just how it is in class. "I can't even sneak a book."

She's looking out the window and worrying. Probably about the man who beat up our dad.

I turn around and pull her in for a hug. "How about

I talk to your teacher?"

"*No.*" Mia pulls back. "Don't tell her anything. I'll do better today."

"You do your best. That's all anybody can ask of you." I smooth down her hair and reach into the laundry basket on my bed. The first thing that comes to hand is a cute black dress with a pattern on it—Minecraft torches. "Change into this, okay? We have to get going."

She scrutinizes the dress, and I hold my breath. If it's another bad day, I've left just enough time to walk them. But everything else has to go right.

Mia takes the dress. Her shoulders droop, and she looks at me with big, sad eyes. "I just don't want to be in trouble today."

"If you do, go to the office and call me. I'll fix it."

I know I can't always fix things. I won't be able to step in every time she has a problem. But today? I can let her teacher know that she needs a little extra patience.

Ben appears in the doorway behind her. "I don't want to go either."

"Because they're out to get me," Mia says.

"Nobody at school is out to get you. I know how hard it is. Okay?" Ben frowns, but I give him an encouraging smile. "I know it sucks having to go to school in a new place. You didn't want to move here. I get it." I sling an arm around both of them, gathering my siblings in. "But this is where we are, and what we need to do now is…"

"Give it a chance," they both say.

"That's right. We need to give it a chance."

Mia leans her head against me for a moment, then straightens up. "Fine. But I'm not doing anything wrong on purpose."

"Try counting to ten before you get up. Just give it another ten seconds. See how it goes today."

Mia slips out of the room to change, but Ben sticks his hands in his pockets. "I can't count to ten and get my old friends back. There's nobody good at the new school."

I run a hand over his hair. "You might not have met them yet, you know. There are good people everywhere. You just have to find them."

Some advice, coming from me. I'm the one who bent over my boss's desk yesterday. Because he made me.

Because I wanted to.

I'm fairly certain that doesn't count as *good*.

"Are we ever going back?"

His green eyes look for sincerity in mine. I've never been able to bullshit Ben. "Honestly? I don't think so. But I don't know. Anything could happen."

"Okay." He sighs, but then he shakes his head like he's getting out of the pool. "I'm going to get my backpack. Do you want anything?"

"I'm all good. But you're sweet." I grab my purse.

My phone. "I just have to talk to Dad before we leave. Check on Mia?"

"Mia," he says through their bedroom door as I go through the apartment. "How hard is it to put on a dress?"

Her laugh is muffled by the door.

Dad's standing by his dresser, going through his wallet. I step in and shut the door most of the way. "I need to talk to you about something."

"What is it, hon? Can't be any bad news, right?" He smiles, optimistic as hell, but his bruise still looks terrible. Nobody's going to give him a job while he looks like that. It *really* needs to hurry up and heal.

"My boss found out."

His hands go still on the wallet. The non-bruised skin on his face pales. "Well, shit. You know I don't have the money, Bristol. I had to use it to pay off that debt."

"Of course." I try not to let my frustration show. My confusion. Because it isn't confusing. It's simple, really, what Mr. Leblanc offered. What he *demanded*. My body as repayment for the money I stole. My body in exchange for staying out of jail. It just *feels* confusing. I shouldn't have liked it. I shouldn't have gotten any pleasure out of it. I should not have thought about it in bed last night. "But you said you'd get a job and help me pay it back."

He promised.

"Yeah." Dad slips his wallet into his back pocket and gives it a pat. Then both hands go into his pockets. "It didn't pan out."

"Dad."

"Hasn't panned out *yet*."

"*Dad*."

"What?" He shrugs, the movement exaggerated. "Guy who owns that company is some rich prick. Why does he care about a measly amount of money?"

"Fifty thousand dollars is not a measly amount of money. I *stole* it. For you. And he has proof that I did it. He could turn me in."

"Bristol, it's not so bad." He puts his grin back on, never mind the black eye. "You just have to be patient."

"Tell that to my boss."

His gaze turns shrewd. "You know…"

You know…

I want to ascend to another plane. Leave my body behind. This is the tone he uses when he thinks he's got a great idea. It's *never* a great idea.

"Dad, no."

"Maybe you can use it to your advantage. Play the helpless maiden card. Men love that."

I throw a glare at him. "I am not having sex with my boss for money."

I could drown in hot shame. I've already agreed to have sex with Mr. Leblanc for money. I let him touch me. I let him take me right to the edge.

And I'll do it again.

I stare down my dad.

He stares back.

I want him to be the one who looks away first, but he doesn't.

"What is your plan? Have you put in any applications?"

My dad shakes his head. "Nobody's going to hire me. I don't have the experience."

"Dad, you have experience in just about everything. You know you can talk your way into a job. *Any* job."

"Bristol, come on. I'm not cut out for most things. I can't work at McDonald's like this. They wouldn't let me. And I don't do well with machines."

He doesn't do well with people, either.

Clearly.

I take the deepest possible breath and let it out slowly. "I did this for the twins. You said you'd help me pay it back."

Silence. He folds his arms over his chest.

"This is it. Do you see that?" I'm tired of the constant fight to make him understand. "You can't keep doing this. It's not good for Mia and Ben."

He scoffs. "This is my work. This is my *life*. What the hell else am I supposed to do?"

"You run cons. And they haven't panned out, have

they?"

His shoulders curve.

"Have they, Dad?"

"Fine." He turns his head, looking vaguely toward the corner of the room. The floor. "The last few times haven't panned out." His eyes come back to mine. They're already lighting up, determined. "That doesn't mean the next one will fail. I just need a little more time."

"That's what you always say, Dad, and it's never a lack of time. It's money. You needed money, and I bailed you out. The next step is for you to get a real job and start paying me back."

The smile disappears from his face. "Jesus. You want money so bad? I'll get some. But you're going to have to wait. I can't pull it out of a hat. I'm not a magician, Bristol."

No. I'm the magician. I'm the one who reached into my job and pulled money out of nowhere for this man.

I swallow rage and betrayal and garden-variety hurt. When are the twins supposed to be safe, living with him? How are they supposed to make it to eighteen without serious damage? Eight years might as well be forever.

"I'm happy to wait. I'd appreciate it if you got started, though. We don't have unlimited time."

I turn my back on my dad and go to find Mia and Ben.

They're both dressed, backpacks on. Mia nudges Ben with her elbow. "I'm not going to get into trouble today. I'm going to be more like you."

Her twin brother gives her his biggest golden-boy smile. "Good. You might be better off that way."

Chapter Ten
Will

I'M ALWAYS THE first one at the office, but this is early. Way too early.

Once again, I couldn't sleep. Nothing helped. Not the gym. Not counting to a thousand. Nothing.

I paced back and forth from my bed to my living room, as if it made any difference. I spent at least an hour staring at the painting my brother Emerson gave me.

If I wanted to downplay who he is, I'd say he was a prominent art collector in the city.

In reality, people know his name all over the world. Dealers and artists fall all over themselves to give him private showings, which are the only ones he'll attend.

Over the years, he's told a few well-connected people in the art scene that he insists on private showings because if he looks at art in public, it fucks with the value. Somebody's always watching to see if he's interested or not interested in a piece.

That's true, but it's not the whole truth. It turns out Emerson didn't need the whole truth to gloss over how rarely he left his house before he met his wife, Daphne. So rarely that when he showed up at my apartment unannounced one day last winter, I thought for a minute I was hallucinating. The fact that he was wearing his winter wetsuit and a packable coat didn't help.

Now he leaves more often, but his visits to Daphne's brother's house or her family's mansion are orchestrated as much as his visits to the city. Carefully planned and scaffolded so he can always get back home.

Anyway. His ability to find pieces that will be worth millions of dollars is legendary. So is his private collection. The painting that hangs in my living room is one of the ones he kept for himself.

It's an original Van Gogh, for fuck's sake. Unmistakably Van Gogh. Lights reflected in the dark water of a canal. A peaceful sky.

I texted him.

Will: *Why the hell would you give me this painting?*

His reply came fast.

Emerson: *You chose it.*
Will: *Are you always awake in the middle of the goddamn night?*
Emerson: *Are you?*

I could picture his expression. My brother's face is a mirror of mine, except the way he sees things is different. It's *more*. When he turns his attention on you, it's like having someone look into your brain and rifle through your thoughts.

His question is sincere.

Emerson: *The painting is like you. That's why you chose it.*

I sent him a laughing emoji instead of *are you kidding me, prick?*

The painting is nothing like me. It's a calm night scene. You can practically feel the people strolling along the canal, smiling gently. I'd be a fistfight reflected in the water.

And even if that *was* the reason I chose it, Emerson had no business giving it to me. Not when it's all a fraud.

So, no.

I couldn't sleep. I couldn't relax. All I could do was want Bristol Anderson. All I could do was count the minutes until she'd be near me again.

It's not an appropriate feeling to have about anyone at the office, but certainly not the temp who stole fifty thousand dollars.

This blackmail game isn't about what I want. It's about making sure she pays for what she took. It's about taking each red cent from her soft skin, her sweet hair, her full lips.

I rub both hands over my face and lean back in my desk chair.

Fine.

I want her.

But not because I think there's anything beyond these two weeks. Nothing between us. There can't be, because Bristol Anderson is a beautiful young woman who made a terrible mistake and I'm barely human.

I just want to fuck her. And hurt her. And destroy her.

There would be nothing left but a sobbing, quivering mess of a woman when I was done with her. She would be appalled if she knew even one percent of the things I want to do. Mark her and bite her and break her. I'm a monster, which is why I'm not letting myself do those things.

I won't hurt her that much if I only fuck her in the confines of the office.

That whisper in the back of my mind calls me a liar. An unconvincing liar. I don't agree with it. If I were to feel things for her, it would be proof that I need her. That I need her to *stay*. I don't do that. I don't need people. I especially don't need Bristol Anderson.

An email notification appears on the screen. It's an invitation. Dinner reservations with Greg Winthrop and Mitchell Hope of Hughes Financial Services tonight.

Reservations, because Hughes Financial Services accepts my demands.

All my demands.

Even the superyacht.

I laugh out loud but there's no humor in it. It has to be a joke, right? Handing over a yacht because some asshole said he wanted it? What kind of world am I living in?

I'm not worth this much. No matter how hard I work or how much money I make, I'm not worth much at all.

But no, it's right here in black-and-white pixels on my large, curved screen. Tonight we'll have dinner and shake hands. The lawyers will draw up the papers.

I accept the invitation. It appears on my calendar a second later.

It hasn't been a full minute when Christa rushes into my office at high speed. It's exactly the velocity I'd expect from a person who's all sharp angles and red lipstick and no-bullshit attitude. "They accepted?"

"Are you just now catching up on all the emails?"

Christa rolls her eyes. "I wasn't up all night like you. I can't *believe* they agreed to buy you a yacht."

"No, let's get this straight. They're begging to buy me a yacht."

"Now all you have to do is *not* fuck it up."

I'm a little offended. "How would I fuck it up?"

She shakes her head. "Of course you didn't look at the guest list on the calendar invite."

"What about it?"

"Apparently Phineas Hughes might actually be coming."

My gaze sharpens. "Really."

"He responded with *Maybe*."

A snort. "More like his secretary responded with *Maybe*. No way is he coming."

Summit has definitely made a splash in New York City. I'm not being humble. I get hammered with interview requests from news outlets and investors wanting the next big secret. I'm still not playing at the level of Phineas Hughes, COO of the entirety of Hughes Industries. I'm a small fish compared to the whale of their Financial Services division. But that division is only a fraction of the overall corporation's total revenue. I don't expect this merger even crossed his desk, much less warranted a dinner.

Christa sits down on the corner of a chair in that way she has, where it seems like it should fall over but doesn't. A glossy black Louboutin taps against the marble floor. "That's what I thought. But then I called over. I used to work with someone in their IP department."

"What? You never told me that."

She folds her hands primly on her lap. "You didn't need to know."

"How long before you broke her heart?" We mostly talk business, both of us being workaholics. But we've worked together long enough that I know a little of her personal life. Enough to rib her constantly for the endless stream of women she makes cry.

"Three weeks. It was a long one. But I'm not taking any shit from you, Mr. Emotionally Unavailable."

I shrug, not minding the retort. "If you don't date them, you don't have to break up with them."

"New York City's most eligible bachelor, ladies and gentlemen."

"So are you going to tell me what your ex said?"

"Well, she spoke to her new flame who works in HR who talked to someone who—it doesn't matter. Apparently, this is on his schedule. His *real* schedule. The one that shows up on his phone. He's going to try and make a drop-in appearance between one event and another."

"If he does, we'll shake hands. No big deal."

"You have a tendency to get punchy." Her gaze gets lost in the middle distance. I can tell she's calculating Summit's new bottom line pending any number of details that will be hashed out after this dinner. "Maybe not literally. You have your little fight nights for that. But you get emotionally punchy."

"Emotionally punchy?"

"Yes. A tendency to push people away. Such as... a

long string of secretaries."

Fuck. Was I emotionally punchy with Bristol? Of course I was, because she stole from me. *You were an asshole before that*, says a small voice in my head. A voice that sounds annoyingly like my brother Sinclair. "Well, it's a good thing I'm not asking Hughes to fetch my coffee tonight."

She raises both hands in the air. "I'm serious. This is yours to lose. You already have the deal, unless you fuck it up. The only thing you can do is make it worse. These guys have to *like* you. They have to be charmed by you. And most of all, they need to be distracted from work."

"It's a work dinner."

"Yeah, but there's the kind of work dinner where you debate ideas, and there's the kind where you talk about where you're vacationing for the winter."

"I'm great at debating ideas, thank you very much. And I don't take vacations. Ever."

"You're great at *winning* debates, but that's not what you need to do with these bigwigs. And definitely not with Finn Hughes. If you piss him off, it's over."

"So you want me to kiss his ass?"

"God, Will, are you trying to sink the deal?"

I'd moved on from it in my head. Focused on Bristol.

Is *she* why the prospect of merging with a megacorp suddenly seems unappealing? It's the obvious next move for Summit. And for me. There's a superyacht, for fuck's sake.

"No," I say, but that's a lie.

I *was* trying to sink the deal. It's why I submitted a real counteroffer that included a yacht. Now I don't know what I'm doing.

Highly unusual.

Christa sobers. "You don't have to be worried. Just… be less yourself."

"It's really a wonder you didn't go into motivational speaking."

She narrows her eyes. "You should probably bring a date."

"Why don't you just come?"

My brilliant CFO laughs out loud. "Because I terrify most men. Except you."

Sure. Except me.

"Anyway, they want to wine and dine you. See how you'll be away from the boardroom."

"I don't care about wining and dining. I care about the bottom line."

I also care about when, exactly, Bristol is going to show up. It's already seven fifteen. Office policy says that everyone has to be here by seven thirty. I feel like I've been waiting months. Years.

"The guys from Hughes *do* care. They want to throw some money around, pay for expensive champagne, and act important. Which is why you need to bring a date."

"I'm married to the business. Feels like cheating."

"That's why we get along." Christa pats at her hair, somehow making her body into even more angles as she does it. "But you're moving up in the world, Will. Bigger than this." She gestures around us. Two floors in a Manhattan office building. "Think CEO of JP Morgan. That's where your future is."

"Yeah. Probably."

She watches me, suspicious. I'd think something was up if I were Christa. I'd think I'd been possessed. I've spent years chasing profits over everything else. I've spent years chasing a merger just like this one.

I'm beginning to wonder if I was wrong. Before Bristol Anderson walked into my office, I'd have taken this ambivalence as a clear sign that I was losing my mind.

Now, all I can see is the other side of the contract and the merger.

The *acquisition.*

What's there that I haven't had already?

A yacht, sure. But imagining the yacht seems empty.

That has nothing to do with the fact that Bristol won't be a temp by the time the deal is finalized. She'll be long gone, working in some other office in the city.

I think about signing that contract and moving forward with no Bristol Anderson, and I don't feel satisfied.

I don't feel giddy.

I feel nothing.

"Okay." Christa's been watching me, and here I am, staring into space. "You can't go to this alone. Not if you're going to zone out and forget you're at dinner."

"Fine. I'll take someone."

She slides her phone out of her pocket and scrolls. Taps. "There are options if you want me to find you a date. I have several people in my network who would definitely make themselves available for you."

"*No.*"

Christa raises her eyebrows.

"I can find a date."

"To be clear, no paid company."

"Get out of my office."

"Email me if you change your mind."

"Goodbye."

On her way out the door, Christa pauses, stepping to the side. "Morning, Bristol," she says.

"Hi." Bristol's in the doorway then in a rose-pink shell and her skirt suit. I could lock us in here for the rest of the day and forget about the dinner entirely. "Good morning, I mean."

She strides across my office, putting my coffee carefully in its place. Bristol has a folder tucked under her arm. It doesn't go onto the desk, however.

Instead, she goes back to the door and closes it. Then

she takes the seat across from me and sits up tall.

"This isn't how you bring the overnight reports, Ms. Anderson."

I'd prefer it if she came and bent over the desk instead.

"I checked your schedule. You have thirty minutes before your first meeting. I just need five of them. There's something I wanted to discuss with you."

"And what's that?"

Bristol pushes the folder toward me, her dark eyes never wavering from mine. "Repayment."

Chapter Eleven
Bristol

Mr. Leblanc looks at me, amusement making his features sharp and cold and beautiful. "We've already discussed repayment. Did you forget?"

No. I haven't forgotten. It's all I can think about, which is why I spent three hours yesterday coming up with the proposal. I spent three hours trying to stay calm.

"I'm only here for two weeks. That won't be enough time to…" I clear my throat. Two weeks is definitely enough time to fuck me in several different ways. I'm sure Mr. Leblanc intends to do it. "To pay off the debt in full. With… with money. With a payment schedule. I can't afford all of it at once, but—"

Mr. Leblanc shifts in his seat at the word *money*, drawing himself closer to the folder. He opens it and scans over the top page. "Absolutely not."

"What I took is… money. I wish I could give it back. I wish I'd never taken it. I'm sorry. So sorry. I want to return what I took... plus interest. That's only fair."

His eyes flick up toward mine, then back to the paper. My chest is tight with the fear that he might laugh out loud... or that he might accept. That he might prefer money rather than blackmailing me.

"I sat down last night and figured out the maximum that I could pay you every month—or weekly, if that's how you wanted it." It's an optimistic schedule. Not impossible, but definitely hard. It's assuming that the temp agency keeps paying me at the same hourly rate. It's also assuming that Dad stops getting into debt. That last one may be what breaks me.

Mr. Leblanc flips the first page and reads through the second. He's handsome this way. It's nice to look at him when he's not cutting into my heart with his sea-glass eyes.

"So you'll be able to pay me back in..." Those eyes follow a column to the bottom edge of the page. "Twelve thousand years."

My face heats. "It's not that long. But I made sure the interest rate was fair."

He huffs, his lips curving in a half-smile. A rare expression for him.

I think he's really entertained by my proposal.

"This is just a hypothetical, Ms. Anderson." Mr. Leblanc pushes the folder across the desk, effectively abandoning it. "And it's fixing a problem you don't have.

I've already told you what I'll accept in return for not having you thrown in jail. Come here."

Is it wrong to be relieved that he wants me closer?

Yes.

The fact that it's wrong doesn't change anything.

I'm nervous. Of course I am. I don't know what he'll do when I get around to the other side of his desk. But I'd be lying if I said I didn't want to get closer.

I'd be lying if I said I didn't want him to touch me.

Mr. Leblanc creates a little more space between his chair and his desk. As soon as I'm within reach, he puts a hand on my waist and pulls me into his lap.

If putting my hands on his desk and letting him touch me was wrong, this is a thousand times worse.

He settles me over him, straddling his lap. I'm lightheaded from lack of oxygen. If anyone walked in before, I could have straightened up. Now, with my thighs spread and my panties brushing the front of his pants…

They'd know.

They'd *see*.

My face goes hotter than the worst sunburn of my life, which I got in ninth grade. I'd gotten a job selling concessions at the city pool and ended up selling bottled pop from a tray.

Eight hours. No hat. You can see how it was.

He guides my palms to the front of his shirt. Through the expensive cloth, I can feel his heart beating.

I'm probably not supposed to ask questions, but...

"Mr. Leblanc, what—" I'm breathless. "What will you do if someone walks in?"

"You can only hope no one does before I'm finished with you." His eyes trace over me, lingering on exposed skin. There's not much of it. I'm dressed appropriately for work. That makes the position feel even dirtier. My skirt. His dress shirt and slacks. "Keep your hands where they are."

I keep my palms over his heartbeat while his hands move.

He pushes my skirt farther up my thighs, then skims his knuckles over the gusset of my panties.

Mr. Leblanc's blue eyes darken. "Interesting. You like paying debts with your body?"

"No. Of course not."

"Then why are you so wet?" he murmurs, and then he leans in and kisses me.

Most people are actually terrible at multitasking, but not Will Leblanc. It's a deep kiss. Confident. Like I owe it to him, which I do.

It's the same way he touches me. Mr. Leblanc pushes the fabric of my panties to the side and strokes me. I've been thinking about him constantly and the real sensation is almost too much to bear. My hips try to tilt away, but he puts a hand at my waist and holds me still.

Okay. I'll stay. I'll stand it. It's pleasure, no matter

how intense it is.

He unbuttons my jacket. Undoes the top button of my shirt, and the second. Reaches under my bra. He tastes my mouth more deeply, and as he does, as I fall into the kiss, he pinches my nipple.

I moan into his mouth.

"Oh," he murmurs. "You liked that." He does it again, and then his fingers are more insistent between my legs. Two fingers push inside me. "You liked it quite a bit, Bristol."

"What, is that—is that not allowed? Do I have to hate it in order to pay you back?"

"Some men might prefer that."

"Not you?"

He pulls back so I can see his eyes. Studies mine. It's a sharp, searching look, and I feel naked underneath it, like he can see through to my heart and all the filthy thoughts in my head.

"To be clear, I'd like to make you cry." A flash in his eyes. He *does* want that. I understand, in a heartbeat, that he's holding back. There's a side of Will Leblanc that he never brings into the office. A dark bedroom, maybe. A locked room. That's where he might let it out. "But you'd enjoy yourself even more."

I shake my head *no,* but he's right. I know he is.

Mr. Leblanc's free hand traces my collarbone. He grips my throat. Short. Glancing. I see it for what it is.

Here's what I'll do before I make you cry. Then he moves his hand to the back of my neck, but he doesn't lean in for another kiss. He holds me still, watching, as he finger-fucks me. Slow and deep.

I understand without asking that I'm not supposed to close my eyes. That I'm not supposed to hide anything from him.

It feels so revealing when he watches me like this. Almost like he'd stripped me naked and put me in front of a spotlight.

"Are you this wet and hungry because I'm your boss?"

I don't know how he can ask me questions in such a level, businesslike tone when he's playing with my body. Testing the depth of his fingers. The pad of his thumb on my clit. Minuscule adjustments. As his temporary secretary, I've seen him do this in email chains. Small, considered changes to investment deals that seem like they should be nothing, but they end up making him millions of dollars.

I didn't know the skill could translate into orgasms.

It's going to, if he doesn't stop.

Please, don't let him stop.

"Yes. No."

"Which is it?"

"I think—" I think my brain is unraveling. Pleasure overload. I don't like to lie, but I don't like to tell all my secrets, either. I just can't help it. "I think it's both. I think it's you."

I'd still think he was gorgeous even if he wasn't my boss. I'd still want him no matter where he worked. Will being my boss is icing on the cake.

"Why do you have a palm tree on your desk?" Mr. Leblanc asks. "Those tropical candies?"

I'm waist-deep in pleasure. Maybe up to my chest. Maybe up to my head. It's warm and bright, like ocean water under the sun. It takes a second for the words to penetrate. "What?"

"On your desk. You have a figurine of a palm tree. And a bowl of candy."

My hands flex on his shirt. "Why were you looking at my desk?"

He did more than look. Mr. Leblanc knew they were tropical Jolly Ranchers, which means he picked one up. Turned it over and read the wrapper. Did he think about how they'd taste?

About how I'd taste?

"I go past it every day on the way out. I can look at my own property whenever I please." I clench around his fingers, and Mr. Leblanc laughs, low and mean. "Dirty. You're my property too, Bristol. I own you until you've paid back your debt. Answer the question."

The question. The palm tree. The candy. "My siblings gave it to me. It's a reminder. So are the candies."

He circles my clit, adding pressure, and I'm really going to come. I'm desperate to know whether he'll let me do it or whether he's just teasing. Just torturing.

"A reminder of what?"

"Of where I—" I almost come mid-sentence. "Where I want to go."

"And where is that?"

"The beach."

"Why do you want to go to the beach, Bristol? You want men to look at you in your bikini. You want them to stare at your tits and wonder what your pussy feels like?"

"I want you to look."

That's when it happens. All the heat and pleasure between my legs exposed. I can't see his face any more. I can only feel his hand on the back of my neck. Can only hear him.

"That's worth some money, Bristol. Keep coming. It's fucking gorgeous. You're making such a pretty mess."

When I come back to myself, I discover that I've made fingernail imprints in the front of his shirt.

And I've done something to him, too. He's lost the reserved, cold expression, and his face is all heat.

Both of his hands go around my neck. Mr. Leblanc kisses me thoroughly, like he can taste pleasure in my mouth.

Then he changes his grip. Hands go to my shoulders.

And he gently, firmly pushes me to the floor between his legs. I'm drawn to him like a magnet. The way his hands work over his belt and his zipper is fascinating.

His cock is freed, and—

I did that. He wants me that much. It's perfect and thick and hard. *So* hard.

"Does it hurt?" I whisper. "For it to be like that?"

"It will hurt less in a minute. You know what to do."

If I wasn't still half-dreaming, still coming down, I might have hesitated to wrap my hand around him. One deep breath, and I lean down and tease the head with my tongue.

Mr. Leblanc groans. "More, Bristol. Now."

Chapter Twelve
Will

THIS IS THE best blow job of my life.

All the other ones fade directly out of my memory. I've dated lots of women. Taken lots of them to bed. There's freedom in a one-night stand, but no one has ever been as enthusiastic and sweet as Bristol.

She's not particularly experienced, but she is *earnest*. It's killing me. My thief of a temp is half under my desk, her skirt still pushed up her thighs, and she cannot get enough of this.

Stay, I want to say.

Stay here. Stay at your desk. Keep bringing me coffee every morning. Put it just the right way on my coaster. Let me fuck you on every break. Let me take you home at night.

Where I'll make you cry and beg and come so hard you pass out.

I don't say anything.

Bristol gives my shaft a long lick, and a shiver goes up my spine to the top of my head.

She couldn't be doing a better job if I was paying her. I put my knuckles over my mouth. Bristol Anderson is destroying the person I've been. I only half-care if anyone on staff hears me.

Bristol responds to a stifled grunt by trying even harder. Giving my cock *more* attention with her lips and tongue.

I've dreamed about this.

More than once.

The dream doesn't come close to reality. The dream didn't include the soft silk of her hair underneath my fingertips. It didn't include the way her cheeks are still pink from coming on my fingers like a perfect corporate whore.

My thighs flex. My cock twitches against her tongue. I concentrate on not coming. I don't want this to be over.

The phone rings.

Not my cell. The big phone on the corner of my desk. The landline.

Bristol looks up at me with her huge green eyes. She's gone completely still except for the heat of her breath over the head of my cock.

I push her head back down and pick up the phone.

"Will Leblanc."

"Have a minute?" It's Greg Winthrop from Hughes Financial Services. One of the people who will be at the dinner tonight. "I wanted to talk to you just briefly about the numbers. I understand your CFO looked them over."

"That's right."

Bristol slows. She adjusts her grip on my base, and then I'm encased in the heat of her mouth again. Slowly, tentatively, she takes me deeper, getting used to me.

"What did you think?"

I didn't care. I should have cared, but I didn't. "I was impressed. Had a couple questions."

What were they? I don't know, because my tip meets resistance at the back of Bristol's throat. I grit my teeth against the absolutely feral sound about to slip out.

"I'd have been surprised if you didn't." He laughs. "This merger stands to put you on a completely different tier. Welcome to the big leagues."

Another scale of wealth entirely. I wouldn't have to do anything else for the rest of my life. I could turn my back on the company. I could coast.

I could take Bristol to the beach. No, that idea is ridiculous. The only reason it occurred to me is because her lips feel so warm around my cock.

"It would be a hell of a change."

"What were your questions?"

I can't think of a single one. She's testing the boundary of her throat now. Shallow thrusts. Seeing how far she can go. Doing her very best, like she has done from the first day. I think of her turning my coffee cup to just the right angle just as she takes me deeper into her throat.

Just the perfect. Fucking. Angle.

Questions. About the merger. About the numbers.

"My main question was actually about the language—" Bristol adds pressure, gagging softly. Tears gather on her eyelashes. I want to fuck her throat when she's bound and helpless and begging. I must sound like I'm having a heart attack. "—concerning the current staff. The policy was too vague. I want a guarantee that Summit can maintain its culture and pay scale. No layoffs. No pay cuts. Nothing."

"I'll review it." Greg's taking notes. "Of course those things will be left to your discretion, but we can come to an agreement on the contract language."

"I want to do right by my employees. That means keeping our systems in place."

"Understood."

My abs bunch up. I plant my feet on the floor and hold her hair tighter. "Nothing else comes to mind, but—"

"If it does, text me. We'll work through it before dinner."

"Perfect."

"We're all looking forward to it. It'll be the perfect time to solidify everyone's preferences. Get comfortable with each other."

Holy fuck, I don't care. I know I'm supposed to be highly invested in the outcome of this dinner, but right now I don't care. I want to leave with Bristol. Abandon everything, including the dinner, and take her to the beach of her goddamn dreams.

"Likewise."

Bristol glances up at me through her lashes with her lips firmly wrapped around my cock. Those eyes glint with a challenge.

My little corporate whore is trying to make me come on this phone call.

She's going to do it if this goes on for another five minutes. Another *two* minutes.

Another one.

Bristol's found a rhythm that's so right it hurts.

"—due diligence," Greg says. I didn't notice him start talking again. "The final negotiations—"

"Will have to be discussed next week." I laugh to cover up how much I want this prick off the phone, now. "I'm sure we can't do that after drinks tonight."

He laughs too. "Of course."

"Call again if something comes to mind before we meet."

"I will. And there was one other—"

"So sorry. My next meeting just walked in the door. Leave a message with my secretary."

The phone barely makes it to the cradle before I have my hands on Bristol.

I had a plan for this. I had a plan for fucking her. I was going to make it hot and humiliating and make her understand, in painstaking detail, what I was taking from her. I was going to drag it out. I was going to make it hurt. I was going to make her cry.

Bristol straddles my lap and I shove her panties to the side. She's trembling, her cheeks red. "Now?"

"Right fucking now."

Those eyes get wider, and I take her face in my hands. "You'll love it. I'll make you love it."

I have to, because I need her. To hell with all my plans.

I put a hand on her hip and guide her down until my tip meets wet flesh. Bristol bites her lip, braces herself on my shirt, and lowers herself down.

"Oh, fuck. You're tight. Keep going."

"I really want this," she murmurs. "I really, really want this."

I can tell she does. She's as earnest as she was when she was sucking my cock. Tight and gripping and *trying*.

"Yes, sweetheart, you do. Fuck. Good work. Take more."

I'm halfway inside her when she starts to lose it. Push harder against me. "I want this," she says again.

Bristol rises up and sinks down *hard,* almost frantic.

She gasps, her hands going to fists on my chest, and I know it must have hurt. My nerves thrill to the startled ache in her eyes. I want to hurt her more. I want to drag desperate sobs out of her. I want her to beg me for mercy. I want her to beg me for everything.

Not yet. Not *yet*.

Bristol's still pulsing around me, caught between pleasure and pain. It's written all over her face. In her wide, green eyes and her parted lips. A silent plea. *Help me.*

The man who belongs in this office would help. He'd still fuck her, but he'd be decent.

I wrap my hands around the back of her neck and kiss her.

"Just stay," I murmur against her mouth. "Stay. For a minute, Bristol. Just a minute."

Her body relaxes into the kiss. She lets me take more of her weight. Sweet tension in her thighs keeps me in place inside of her. Bristol doesn't lift away.

She's staying.

I lick her bottom lip, and her sweet cunt tightens around me. She shivers, but then—before she's ready, I'm sure of it—she starts to rock her hips.

"Better," she says. "Oh, that's better."

She's hotter and wetter every second.

She'd be even wetter if I hurt her. Punished her. Took her past her limits.

Yes.

Fuck my plans for staying still and being gentle. I use one hand to bring her down closer, harder, and fuck her. A knuckle on her clit. The orgasm comes on fast and she buries her face in my shoulder to stifle the noise when she comes.

"Mr. Leblanc," she says. "Oh…"

I lose it when she bites into my shirt. Lose it at the sound of her moans through cotton and skin. I grip her hips with both hands and pull her down. Three deep thrusts and I pin her against me.

I haven't come this hard in years. Ever. Shadows at the edge of my vision. Pressure everywhere. A one-two punch.

"Stay." I can't stop myself from saying it anymore than I can stop myself from spilling inside her. "Stay, Bristol."

I am, she answers. I think. I can't hear. I can't see. I'm distantly aware of throwing my arms around her and holding her close. Distantly aware of her sweet, panting breaths.

On the inside, I'm battered. I've lost control. Gone against every instinct. I made things soft for her when it should have been awful. I made it mean something when it should have been nothing.

It's just the sex. My blood pressure gone haywire. My thoughts. My brain.

This isn't who I am.

I hold her for far too long.

Anyone could walk in, but I can't bring myself to force her away.

Let them walk in. Let them find us here. Have the board remove me from the company. Throw us both out, together.

Yeah. I've lost it.

Eventually, Bristol picks up her head. We untangle ourselves from each other. She cleans herself up with a tissue from my desk, then turns back to face me, face red.

"Was there anything else you wanted?" A moment's hesitation. "Mr. Leblanc?"

"You're coming with me to dinner tonight."

"What?" Bristol's smile wrinkles her nose. "We can't go to dinner together."

"It's a corporate dinner. I'm merging Summit with a company called Hughes Financial Services, and they want to take me out to celebrate. You're coming with me."

"What happens after you merge with them?" The smile has faded from her face. "Do you stay here, or go somewhere else?"

"You'll be gone by then."

I see the realization set in. We're down to eight days. Six business days. They're going to go fast, and then she'll be out of my life. If I didn't make her go, she'd leave anyway. That's always how it is.

"Understand, Bristol, I'm not giving you a choice. I'm blackmailing you, and you're coming to dinner as my date. You're going to be beautiful and charming and sit next to me all evening. Wear something nice."

Chapter Thirteen
Bristol

MR. LEBLANC SENDS a car to pick me up for dinner, which is good, because I don't want to wear my dress on the bus with its questionable floors and cracked plastic chairs. It's a relief to sink into the leather seat and let him drive me away from the apartment complex.

A guilty relief. I'm leaving Mia and Ben with my dad for the evening.

Then again, I have an obligation to do whatever Mr. Leblanc says.

Then again…

I *want* to do this with him.

The fact that I have anything at all to wear is a stroke of incredible luck. I ducked into a department store on the way home from the office. They had a clearance sale section and a dress in my size. Floor-length. Black. An elegant slit.

It would get some looks on public transportation, I

think. I'd have to be extra vigilant about who was around me if I didn't want to get groped. I'm not in a good state of mind for that.

My mind is too crowded with Mr. Leblanc. Then again, I probably will end up groped tonight.

By Mr. Leblanc.

His whole body came alive when he took me. Granted, I was coming all over him at the time. I didn't know how it would feel to have a man inside me. I didn't understand how good it would be. There was pain, but I wanted it. Wanted *him*.

And what he wanted…

To be clear, I'd like to make you cry.

They're the words of a man who likes rough sex. Who likes intensity. And it *was* intense, fucking him in his office chair with the rest of his staff outside. At the end, when he held me down against his body, it felt real. Like the real Will Leblanc had taken control. Like the man at the office is an illusion.

His eyes went dark—blank—when he reminded me of the two-week limit on this arrangement. *You'll be gone by then.*

Gone by the time his merger goes through.

It's going to go through. He said this was a celebration dinner, and it's not going to go wrong because of me. Because my mind is elsewhere. I practice concentrating as we pull up to the curb.

Mr. Leblanc is waiting across the sidewalk, half-turned, when the driver opens my door for me.

I step out of the car, and Mr. Leblanc's face lights up. For a fraction of a second he looks young. Delighted. It's the happiest I've ever seen him, but his expression darkens. Then he blinks, and he's serious again. Calculating. The way he is in the office.

He strides across the sidewalk and offers me his arm. "You look beautiful."

"I—" I'm about to make excuses for the dress, but I don't. "Thank you. Who are we meeting?"

"Greg Winthrop and Mitchell Hope. They're the top people at the company."

"Did *they* bring dates?"

"No. You're the only one."

We go into the restaurant. Fancy. Not so fancy that I feel like I wandered behind a velvet rope I shouldn't have. Mr. Leblanc guides me to a table by a huge circular window looking out over the city. "Greg, Mitchell, this is Bristol. She helps me in the office. Bristol, this is Greg and Mitchell."

Greg has sandy hair and an easy smile. Mitchell has dark hair and permanent frown lines.

"Pleased to meet you," I say with a shy smile.

We all sit down. I'm between Mr. Leblanc and Greg, directly across from Mitchell. A waiter comes to pour wine. I get the impression they've already ordered, but as the men finish a conversation about zoning in Manhattan, a waiter bends down next to me.

Oh, jeez. What am I supposed to order at this dinner? Something small? Something expensive? We didn't talk about that, and I was too busy thinking about the sex to Google the menu. I was too busy thinking about how the first man I ever fucked is my boss, and we did it at work, and there was nothing romantic about it. Nothing romantic except how much he wanted it.

Except for those flashes of longing in his eyes. Except for the way he wanted me to *stay*.

The waiter murmurs something in my ear about the steak.

That's usually expensive, but I'm supposed to be Mr. Leblanc's date. He's rich. I can't give them the impression that he's not. Or that his girlfriend isn't used to eating meals that cost more than five dollars.

I agree to the steak. Medium-well.

"—plans for after the merger is completed? Take some time off?"

Mr. Leblanc blinks, and an easy smile slides onto his face. It's wild to see it. He's never seemed like the easy-smile kind of guy. Now that I've seen it, I want to see it again. After that, I want to see a genuine smile. Hear a laugh that's not controlled or calibrated. "I haven't thought much about it."

"Too busy making money." Mitchell slaps his hand

on the table and laughs. "You'd travel. You'd have to. After the initial breaking-in period, of course. Plenty to do in a place like Amsterdam."

"Sure," Mr. Leblanc says.

"One of my buddies has a condo in the Netherlands. Can't understand why he insists on keeping it. Property can't be improved anymore, but he won't leave." Mitchell steeples his fingers. "I might look at some properties in the South of France when we're there for the holidays."

"Visiting family?" Mr. Leblanc asks.

"Checking on one of my vacation homes." Mitchell looks pointedly at Mr. Leblanc, like he's also about to own a vacation home in the South of France. Maybe he already does. "A real investment piece."

"I could stand to own more property, but you know me." Mr. Leblanc actually sounds sincere. "I think ideas are more interesting. A little cash infusion is all they need to grow."

"Speaking of vacations." Greg smiles at me. It's genuine. "What about you, Bristol? Have you had any time to travel?"

My face goes hot. I'm Mr. Leblanc's date. Anyone he would normally date would travel. They'd probably go to Paris, Rome, and Tokyo. "Mostly across the country."

"Really?"

I pause for a heartbeat in case they want to steer the

conversation away from me. No one interrupts. "I was born out in Arizona. My dad's got a serious case of wanderlust, so we've been making our way east since I was about ten. I told him if we go any farther, we'll end up in the ocean."

"The heat in Arizona is something else," Greg says. "It's so dry. Any plans to go abroad?"

"I don't have any properties to visit." I follow it with a sheepish grin, and Greg and Mitchell laugh.

"That's why they have hotels. Have you ever been to Paris? It's a cliché to stay near the Eiffel Tower, but I have a place with a view. It's a good way to pass the time. Especially with the right company."

Out of the corner of my eye, I catch Mr. Leblanc scowling. He tries to hide it, but I can tell from the set of his mouth that he's not thrilled with Greg's attention on me.

"Actually, if I was going to travel, I'd like to go to the beach."

A moment of silence. Every man at the table looks at me expectantly.

"Which beach?" Greg prompts gently.

"I read about a white-sand beach in the Bahamas that's supposed to be one of the most beautiful in the world." I have that brochure tucked inside a book on my bedside table.

"Not interested in spending more time in the city?"

"I just think it would be fun to take my siblings somewhere warm during the winter. I'm not too picky about the location, though. I'd settle for Florida. I'd settle for anywhere if we could hang out in the sand and swim. It sounds wonderful."

And be away from my father. That would be important. Or maybe he'd come with us, but in my imaginary beach, there would be no cons and no debts. There would be no scary men with guns breaking into our apartment. Instead there'd be a gentle breeze and endless water.

"Siblings?"

I'm probably talking too much. This dinner isn't supposed to be about me. It's supposed to be about Mr. Leblanc and the merger. "I have twin siblings, Mia and Ben. They turned ten this year."

Mitchell's face brightens. "Kids that age are interesting. Some of them have damn good ideas."

"Twins," Greg says. "Wow. Are you close with them?"

"They're my favorite people." Also true. Everybody at the table wears a soft expression. Indulgent, almost. Like me and Mia and Ben are the cutest thing they've ever heard of. "Mia loves to read. Ben's been top of his class in math since kindergarten. They find common ground with video games."

"Well," Greg says as the waiter returns to fill our

water glasses. "If you ever decide on a specific destination, let me know. I can share my contacts. I know at least ten people on every continent. They can find you a good property to rent that's away from the tourist hotspots."

"Oh, thank you. That's so kind. I don't know if I'll ever have the time, but you never know."

"Why not? Does this guy have anything to do with it?" Mitchell nods at Mr. Leblanc. "He should be taking you to the Bahamas *and* Paris. Remember, I've seen his balance sheets."

Mr. Leblanc slings his arm around the back of my chair. "She's indispensable to me at the office."

Greg raises his eyebrows. "You can't let her go, even for a week?"

"Absolutely not." Mr. Leblanc's smiling again, but there's a danger in it now. "I couldn't do anything without a good secretary. Nobody has been better than Bristol."

Greg's eyes dart between the two of us. "I hope you give this woman enough paid vacation."

"Nope," he says smoothly, which is accurate. Due to the nature of temp work, there are no benefits. No paid vacation, that's for sure. Even if I had the money to go anywhere.

"I'm *sure* I'll go," I cut in, challenging Mr. Leblanc with a smile. "Eventually."

He looks back at me. "You're right. You have options."

The smile he gives me makes me hot head to toe. *Options* sounds filthy coming from him. He can't possibly mean anything by it other than fucking in the office. He doesn't mean we should take a vacation together.

Though I would love to see him in swimwear.

Or less than swimwear.

"You could take a work trip," Mitchell suggests. "Work poolside. Started doing that years ago."

"I can work on a tropical beach." Mr. Leblanc's still looking at me. Emotions glint in his blue-green eyes, one after the other. They're gone before I can name them. "The shareholders would probably be glad if I took a week to go email-only. They'd consider it a gift."

"Every CEO needs time to relax." Greg is sage about this. Knowing. I almost laugh out loud. CEOs don't need additional vacations. It's everybody who works for them who needs more time off.

At least, that's what I usually think. Mr. Leblanc's different. Bound up tight. Always tense. He always looks like he's ready to break into a run, or a fight, and the only thing containing his energy is his thousand-dollar suit. Maybe he *does* need a break.

"I wouldn't know," Mr. Leblanc says, and the other men laugh.

We finish eating dinner and sit with espressos and coffee as the evening winds down.

There's a rustling from behind me.

The men's attention is drawn.

Greg smiles wide in a fawning way. Mitchell looks grim, as if he's facing some dark task. And Mr. Leblanc looks impassive. That's how I know that whoever is coming up behind me is important.

Very important.

I turn to see a handsome man, younger than the three at the table, but somehow more powerful. It's something in his stride. In his confident smile. This is someone who knows his place in the world is high. High enough that he can afford to be lenient with the rest of us.

"Hughes." Greg stands up and clasps the man's arm in an effusive shake. "So good of you to come by. Mitchell here thought you might not make it. I told him you would. This deal is important to Hughes Financial Services. A real boon for us."

"Call me Finn." Hughes's voice is kind, but still authoritative. "Outside the office."

Greg chortles, pleased with the offer. Clearly, there are different tiers of *rich*. These men are powerful and wealthy in their own right. They're important enough within the company to sign off on a billion-dollar acquisition agreement. But they're still far below this man.

Hughes. I have a faint recollection of hearing about the Hughes family. People talk about them the same way they talk about the Vanderbilts. Phineas Hughes is the oldest son of the primary branch, the one with a playboy persona.

He doesn't look like a playboy right now, not with his hazel eyes assessing.

Mitchell shakes his hand.

Then it's Mr. Leblanc's turn. They're introduced, and Mr. Leblanc gives a respectful nod. "Hughes."

"Leblanc," he says. "Nice to see you again."

The men look surprised, but Mr. Leblanc tilts his head toward Finn. "He's engaged to my sister-in-law. Congratulations, by the way."

Finn flashes a charming smile. "It seems your brother and I have something in common. A fascination with Morelli women."

I didn't know Will had any siblings.

"What's interesting is seeing my brother fascinated with anything but art." He gestures to me. "This is Bristol Anderson. She works with me at Summit."

Then those hazel eyes turn on me. I'm struck. Mesmerized. He's *handsome.* No wonder he has a bazillion dollars. People probably sign over their life's savings when he looks at them. There's a glint in his eyes that says he knows well his effect on people. It amuses him, though. He gives me a lopsided smile. "Ms. Anderson. A pleasure to meet you."

"And you, sir."

"Finn." There's laughter in his voice. "And unlike these guys, you can call me Finn anytime."

The other men laugh, but Mr. Leblanc tenses beside me. It's just a joke, but he's possessive. Or protective. It's only because I'm the diamond ring in a pawn shop. My only value is my body. But it's hard not to imagine what it would be like in real life, if he were really dating me.

"We'll see how I feel after the deal goes through, Mr. Hughes." I keep my tone frosty with playful reproach. It's a game, that's all. And Mr. Leblanc should see that.

Finn's gaze turns speculative. "You want him to accept, then?"

I glance back at Mr. Leblanc's face, but his expression gives nothing away. "I'm sure he'll make the right decision for himself and for Summit Equity."

Finn gives Mr. Leblanc a sideways glance. "You trust him, then?"

"Yes." I'm surprised to find that I can be honest about this. The medium-well steak and the talk about faraway vacations? Those felt like someone else. But this feels like me. "I trust him."

"He's right here," Mr. Leblanc says, his voice wry.

Finn spears him with a glance. It's not precisely friendly, but it's also not negative. Challenging, I would say. He's giving Mr. Leblanc a challenging glance. "And what about you? Do you trust yourself?"

Mr. Leblanc gives him a hard look. "My results speak for themselves."

"They were particularly impressive on that ODM software."

"Hughes Industries has experience with that. I did a paper on your father in college."

"I know." The corner of Finn's mouth turns up. "I read it."

I feel Mr. Leblanc's surprise. And that he's flattered, despite himself. "Did your father read it?"

There's a slight hesitation in Finn. So slight I almost think I imagined it. "He signed the offer, didn't he? We want Summit to be part of Hughes Financial Services."

"Why?"

"To make money," Finn says.

"You have money."

"To make jobs."

"You employ tens of thousands of people."

"Hundreds of thousands of people," Finn corrects. "Counting our subsidiaries."

"Then give me a real reason." The words are harsh, almost angry.

Greg gasps softly behind us.

"Mr. Leblanc," I say, putting a hand on his arm.

"It's okay, Bristol." Finn isn't bothered in the slightest. "The man has a right to know. Doesn't he? The truth is, I want Summit because of you. But you know that, don't you? And that's why you've hesitated on the deal. You don't want to be bought and sold like a commodity."

Mr. Leblanc glances at me, and I know he's thinking about the debt. "Who would?"

"I'm going to be honest with you." Finn stands tall. "You already know the advantages to the deal. And the many, many commas in the price. But you will be expected to serve Hughes Financial Services, and even Hughes Industries as a whole. Don't take the deal unless you're ready to take orders."

I can't imagine Mr. Leblanc taking orders. Not from anybody. Even someone like Finn Hughes. The air around us simmers with male challenge. There are two alpha wolves, each one clad in fine wool and bespoke shoes. There's a silent battle happening. A vicious one. And it won't be over until one of them wins.

Chapter Fourteen
Bristol

After Finn leaves, the four of us linger for a few more minutes. Then we walk outside together. More handshakes. More smiles. More promises to talk very, very soon. Then Mitchell and Greg climb into waiting cars, and they're whisked away into the night.

Mr. Leblanc's driver pulls up next, but he takes a step back. His brow furrows. He obviously doesn't want to get into the SUV.

"Mr. Leblanc?"

"Let's walk."

"Home?"

"Around the block." His voice brims with tension and energy. It buzzes off him like there was no wine with dinner, only coffee. It's almost the way he sounded when he said *Stay. For a minute, Bristol. Just a minute.* Except now he's practically bristling. Is it excitement or anger? Probably both, from that appearance by Finn Hughes.

"That sounds good."

He offers me his arm, and as soon as I take it, he's moving. Mr. Leblanc waves off his driver and leaves the restaurant behind. After a few paces, he takes his phone out of his pocket, taps out a text, and pushes it back out of sight.

My cheap high heels aren't made for walking. My dress isn't quite enough for the chill of the evening. But I'd walk ten blocks if he asked. I hardly feel the cold. I'm warm. Happy. Full. Maybe it's the wine and the food, or maybe…

Maybe it's that I got to see a different side of Mr. Leblanc tonight. He's not the cold CEO or the dominating sex partner, but a man who can think and laugh and dream.

I steal a glance at him out of the corner of my eye. I might be using him for balance more than I strictly need to. It's not my fault that two glasses of wine went to my head.

Two, or was it three? It was great wine. Smooth and expensive. Nothing I'd ever buy for myself.

Mr. Leblanc looks straight ahead, scanning the sidewalk and the street. He doesn't glance back. He doesn't look like a man whose dreams have just come true.

Is this Mr. Leblanc's dream? Merging with another company and sailing away on a yacht, returning only for meetings with people like Finn Hughes? Vacation properties in Europe, far away from everything he knows?

It must be. Someone like Mr. Leblanc can do lots of things.

He could do anything, really.

The other men at the table, Mitchell and Greg, liked him. Not in a fake way, either. They wanted to hear his opinion on their vacation houses and their plans for the winter. By the end of the meal, they were trying to one-up each other on who could impress Mr. Leblanc with the better vacation story.

That, and Greg was flirting with me. He tried a few more times to invite me to a beach, maybe in France, and eventually I resorted to big smiles instead of turning him down.

Mr. Leblanc was the real star of the show, anyway. He was smart and funny and sometimes even kind.

And then Finn Hughes showed up.

The one thing I'm not sure of is whether Mr. Leblanc can *take orders*, like Finn wanted. I held my breath waiting for Mr. Leblanc's reaction. But he only nodded. Smiled. Shook Finn's hand.

We pass by a bar. The neon sign casts a pink glow onto the sidewalk, and we cross through it as a pair of shadows.

"I think that went well," I offer. Mr. Leblanc's been too quiet to be happy, but he should be. Those guys are thrilled about the merger.

He grunts. I wonder if it's tiring for him to be so charming. I wonder if all he wants right now is to walk far enough to settle his mind so he can climb into bed.

I wonder if he wants more.

"I'm serious. I think they really liked you. They especially liked your ideas about intellectual property. What you said about valuation. I didn't really understand the whole thing, but Mitchell said it was revolutionary." *That's exactly the kind of thinking we need at our company*, he added.

Mr. Leblanc makes another noncommittal sound.

This time, I don't try to hide that I'm looking at him. His eyes are still locked straight ahead. The relaxed expression he wore through dinner has become something else. Like he's thinking too hard about what is obviously a good move for him. Rich men have only one job, and that's to get richer.

"So…" I squeeze his arm. He leans into it a little. I'm not sure he's conscious of doing it. "It's what you want, right? This deal, I mean."

"I don't know." A slight shrug. "Maybe. I thought so, but now there are other things I want."

"Like what?"

"To fuck you until I die."

It hits me like all of New York's heat waves compressed into one. "That's a really long time."

"Is it?" He stops, turning to face me, and I'm surprised at the darkness in his eyes. He's conflicted. Angry. "Or is two weeks just a bullshit amount of time?"

My mouth drops open. "Two weeks is just… that's what my contract is for. That's what it's always like at the agency. A couple weeks. A month."

Mr. Leblanc shakes my hand off his arm like I'm the one who decided on two weeks and not his own company. "I didn't like the way you were flirting with him."

I can't believe he's saying this. "I was making conversation."

"You told him you'd be in touch about a vacation. I'm surprised you didn't leave with him after he offered to let you stay at his place in Paris. You'd probably love the Left Bank."

"You know I didn't mean that. You *know* it."

"You stole fifty thousand dollars from me, but you want me to believe you're above fucking him for a vacation in Paris?"

"Are you serious?" Is this what it feels like to get blown away in a gust of wind? What the hell is even happening right now? My heart thuds. "Even if I wanted to—to fuck him for a free vacation, how am I supposed to *get in touch*? It was just a thing people say. Like hey, I know a great travel agent, and I'm like, yeah, that would be great, thank you. When in reality I'm never going anywhere."

Mr. Leblanc laughs. Cold. Acerbic. He pulls out his phone. "I've got his number right here. Want it?"

"No."

"It doesn't matter. He knows you work with me. For the next week, anyway. He can call you at your desk and the two of you can keep flirting."

"Mr. Leblanc. *Stop*. I didn't even like that guy. I don't want him to call me. I don't want to go to Paris with him."

"You'd prefer the Bahamas, then."

"I don't want to go anywhere with him."

A cold breeze brushes across the back of my neck and ruffles Mr. Leblanc's hair. "Then you should have remembered that at dinner. I'm the one blackmailing you. You stay with *me*."

"I don't know what you're—"

"You flirt with me. Not some asshole from Hughes Financial Services. Not even Finn Hughes."

"Mr. Leblanc…"

Now his grin turns sardonic and mean. Hurt. Disappointed. How can he be disappointed? I did everything he asked. I bought a dress. I sat through dinner. I *charmed*.

"It's not even a surprise. This is what women do. They leave. But guess what, Bristol? You can't leave. You owe me, and your ass is mine until I'm done with you.

You can fuck it up by flirting with other men if you want, but I wouldn't recommend it. I don't think you'd like being locked in."

I'm checking my chest for a knife when I realize he's walked away.

Mr. Leblanc disappears around the next corner before I can get over my shock.

I keep waiting for him to come back. He's not going to *abandon* me here. He's not going to leave me on the sidewalk.

That's exactly what he does.

I'm torn between chasing after him and waiting for him to return, but Mr. Leblanc doesn't come back.

Five minutes pass. The night air starts to feel cold. I can still see the lights from the restaurant. A few couples and groups pass me by. It feels perfectly safe, but painfully lonely. All I want is for one of the pairs of headlights to be his. All I want is for him to come back around the corner, apologizing for being an asshole and promising to take me home with him.

I'm not sure what I'd do then. I want the chance to tell him off, but more than that, I want to know what made him say those things. What made him *think* those things. Greg was pleasant and clearly interested in me, but he was nothing compared to Mr. Leblanc.

Mr. Leblanc was all I thought about all through dinner. The heat of him a short distance away. The sounds he made in his office. The raw, intimate moments we had together.

It's so embarrassing to stand there on the sidewalk that I start walking, not paying attention to the direction. A girl's allowed to wallow in confused heartache for a few blocks.

I've only made it to the next intersection when a car pulls up alongside me. It's the same one Mr. Leblanc sent to bring me to the restaurant. Same driver. He jumps out to the curb. "Ms. Anderson, I'm here to take you—"

"No need."

"Mr. Leblanc sent me to—"

A city bus rattles down the street. "I'll get home by myself. Thank you for coming, but I don't need a ride."

I turn my back on him and head for the bus stop, digging into my clutch purse for emergency fare. I wasn't supposed to need a ride home. I was supposed to be with Mr. Leblanc.

Instead I climb onto the bus and sit in one of the hard plastic seats.

It's crowded with people, but I feel totally alone.

Chapter Fifteen
Will

LAST NIGHT SHOULD have been one of the best nights of my life.

It was one of the worst.

Physically, things were fine. Good. Fucking great. I ate fancy food next to a beautiful woman. I went home to a luxury apartment with two layers of paid security patrolling the lobby and blessed silence when I closed the door. No one was waiting to punch me in the face or shut me in a closet.

Many nights were like that growing up. Hungry. Violent. And I was the lucky one. My older brothers did their damned best to distract our father. To get in his way before he could get to me.

It was a nightmare in comparison to the dream I'm living now. Top one percent. A goddamn superyacht on the way.

A living nightmare.

But nothing came close to the constant hope and constant disappointment around my mother.

I thought she would come back.

Of course I thought she would. That's what mothers are supposed to do. Come home. I imagined that when she did, she would be beautiful and kind and rescue us from our father. All my hope was built from a vague memory of a woman singing a song.

I can't be sure that the voice in my memory is hers at all. It could be something I heard on the radio or TV. It's not clear enough to identify. Not the tune. Not the words.

Just hope like a deep, spreading bruise. Hope that was beaten down again and again and again until we finally left home. By then, I knew how fucking pathetic it was to wish she'd come back. My mother is dead. Even if she were still alive, I wouldn't recognize her.

Eight a.m., and I'm sitting behind my desk at Summit, an email response open on my computer screen.

It's from one of the guys in the finance department. Yet another email about money.

Everything has to do with money.

How have I let this dominate my life?

What I want most is Bristol.

I was an asshole last night. It made me feel like I was on fire to watch her flirt with that prick Greg. It made me feel like my stomach was sinking into the ground.

Abandoned, all over again. Foolish, all over again. Pathetic.

I want her for sex. That's all. I want her for what we agreed on. I want her where she's supposed to be.

I want her here, where I can see her.

And every minute she's not here, the bruising fear grows. A creeping, anxious feeling. She left. She's gone. She's never coming back.

It'll stop when she shows up at the door.

She's usually here by now with my coffee and a determined smile.

"Bristol," I shout toward the door. I hope it'll work like magic. Say her name once, and she'll be here.

Instead, there's a whispered conversation outside. Then one of the analysts steps in.

"Bristol won't be here today, Mr. Leblanc. She called in. Something about a storm and a roof problem."

"A *roof* problem?"

"That's what she said, yes."

The analyst is bracing herself like I'm going to lose my mind. I might, but not here.

I might, because Bristol is obviously lying. She didn't like how the dinner went, and she didn't like being blackmailed. She did what women always do, which is leave.

Well, fuck that. I'm not going to allow her to leave. And if she's going to try, she's not going to do it with some bullshit excuse about a roof.

I stand up, and the analyst's eyes get huge. "Mr. Leblanc?"

Keys. Wallet. "Cancel all the meetings on my schedule."

"But—" She probably doesn't know how to cancel my meetings. This woman doesn't have access to my calendar. I don't care. "You're leaving?"

"Yes."

The analyst follows me out of my office and watches me go. They're all silent by the time I reach the elevators. I can feel them staring. I can feel their shock.

Me, leaving the office on a Friday morning.

Me, canceling a day's worth of meetings.

It's never happened before.

I find Bristol's address from the man I paid to get information on her. Five minutes, and I'm on my way.

I drive through neighborhoods that are progressively shittier until my phone notifies me that I'm within a quarter mile of her address. The block is made up of convenience stores with dirty awnings and, finally, Bristol's apartment complex.

I park my car in front of a broken VISITOR PARKING sign and scan the addresses on the buildings. Bristol's is at the back of a courtyard. Building C.

The courtyard is as busted up as the front door of the building, which is dented to shit. There's no doorman.

It's not even locked. Inside a decrepit room that can be charitably called the lobby, the elevator's *out of order.* The sight of the chain across the doors and the dangling sign sets my teeth on edge. After her days working as a temp, Bristol doesn't even get a few moments to relax in the elevator.

I take the stairs. Three floors up. My heart rate is fast and pissed and scared when I get to the landing. I know her apartment will be empty. She'll be gone, gone, gone.

The door creaks when I pull it open and reveal Bristol's hallway.

It's a disaster. Garbage bags are piled in the hallway, and one of the doors is open.

I hear her inside before I reach it.

I push it a little farther with my fingertips and find absolute chaos.

Roof problem was an understatement. The apartment was trashed. Chunks of plaster everywhere. The living room is soaked. The TV is lying facedown in the middle of the carpet, obviously broken.

"Bristol." It comes out more like it would at the office. Brusque and irritated.

She hurries out of a side room, a clear garbage bag dangling from her hand. Her dark hair is pulled into a bun at the top of her head. Her cheeks flush when she sees me. "What are you doing here?"

"What the hell happened?"

I don't say *I didn't believe you.* I don't say, *I didn't think you were coming back. And you know what? That would have been the right thing to do. I don't deserve to touch you.*

Bristol's shoulders sag. "This happened. The roof caved in during the storm last night."

I barely noticed the storm last night. There were a few moments of loud rain on the windows of my apartment. It was background noise in my clean, spacious two-bedroom with my original Van Gogh and my custom furniture and carpet so soft you could lie on it for hours, if you had to.

"Where are the twins?"

Her eyes come up to mine, and I can see her wondering if I'm going to fire her. I can see her debating whether to bring up last night and the way I left her standing there on the sidewalk.

Leaving her before she could leave me.

Regret is an arm locked around my neck. Knuckles colliding with my stomach. I can't undo it. I can never undo it. Walking away is always final.

But I could try. I could try, if she lets me stay.

Bristol should refuse to answer me. She should kick me out of this destroyed apartment. I brace for it. Accept it before it can hurt.

Her shoulders let down. "I sent them to school. It was dry, at least. They had enough clothes to get through the day. It's better for them to be there while I pack everything up."

"And your father?"

"He already took his things and left. He bails whenever things get tough. I have to find us another place to live. The management isn't going to rush to fix this for us."

"Why wouldn't they? Do you not pay rent on time?"

"Because it's a sublet. We're not even really on the lease. Somehow, this is going to come back on us, and then—" A deep breath, and she turns away. "I just need to get our things together and figure out a plan before the twins get out of school. I'm sorry I called in, Mr. Leblanc. I told them how you take your coffee."

"Fuck the coffee."

Bristol steps out of sight. I follow her through the natural disaster of the living room and into a tiny bedroom. It's barely large enough to hold a twin bed and a basket. I recognize some of her clothes, folded neatly. The dress she wore to dinner last night is draped over the dresser.

The bed's already been stripped. Blankets and sheets are in another clear garbage bag on the floor. Bristol kneels on the bare mattress, taking something down from the wall. A postcard held in place by a thumbtack. She handles it gently, like a work of art, and tucks it into a book.

The book goes into the garbage bag.

"Why are you here, Mr. Leblanc?" Bristol looks over her shoulder at me. She looks tired and sad and still so beautiful. "To yell at me? I don't think I can take it. To fuck me?"

"No. I'm taking care of this."

"Taking care of what?" A despairing laugh. "You know how to fix a broken ceiling?"

"I know people who can fix a broken ceiling. I also know people who can clean this up. They'll start work as soon as we've cleared out your personal things."

"Do you know people with a spare storage unit that they'll let me use for free?"

"Yes. And I have room at my place for everything else."

"You shouldn't have to do this." She's embarrassed. "My dad didn't even pretend to try. I don't know if he's planning to come back at all."

"Don't worry about him. We'll finish packing. We can pick up Mia and Ben early, if you don't want them to have to come back here."

It's a dire situation. I didn't realize just how dire until I was standing in the middle of it.

I know, because I recognize this place. Our house was often the site of a natural disaster growing up, except the natural disaster wasn't a storm. It was my father. The fifty thousand dollars she took doesn't mean anything to me. I really could have spent it on coffee, if I'd wanted to.

It's a fortune to Bristol.

And she used absolutely none of it on this apartment. Not on furniture. Not on the cheap dress she wore to dinner. Not on making it better for herself. All of that went to keeping a roof over her siblings' head.

Anger heats my chest. Bristol would have been better off if she'd taken the money for herself. She could have used it to rent another apartment. Escape. Anything.

I'm furious with her father. I'm furious with myself. But I understand her. I can't look at her like a corporate whore. I can't look at her like a woman who will leave. She doesn't leave when it counts, even though she should.

"Where are the bags?"

Bristol eases herself down from the bed and stands in the center of the room. It's so small that I could reach out and touch her. "Are you sure about this? I know you have meetings at the office."

"I canceled the meetings. This is more important."

"Nobody—" She swallows. "Nobody can fix this overnight. If you know of a cheap hotel, or somewhere—"

"You'll stay with me. I don't care if it takes a week. I don't care if it takes two."

That's longer than she's supposed to work for me, and we both know it.

Bristol's face softens. "You're not mad?"

"Did you learn how to create storms and use your power to destroy your apartment roof just to get back at me for being a jackass? I'd deserve it."

She cracks a smile. "No."

"Then point me to one of those bags. I'll pack up the next room."

Chapter Sixteen
Bristol

Mr. Leblanc's driver takes me to Mia and Ben's school to pick them up, and it's more than a little weird, waiting in the carpool line in a fancy SUV. The final bell rings, and kids pour out of the front entrance. They all run down the steps like they barely survived. Like they can't wait to be free in the sun.

Mia and Ben are walking a little slower than the rest.

We were all up most of the night. It would probably have been best for them to sleep, but the apartment had to get cleared out. It was much drier at school.

Mia picks up her head as they reach the bottom step and sees me standing by the black SUV. Her eyes fly open wide. Then they're both sprinting to me, colliding in a hug.

"Is that your car?" she asks. "What's going on?"

"It's my boss's car." I could tell them a white lie and say that Mr. Leblanc is my friend, but he's not. He's never been my friend. "We're going to be staying at his place while the apartment gets fixed."

I usher them into the car. When we're finished buckling up, I find Ben staring at me.

"Your boss's apartment?" He says this like I announced we'd be living on the moon until the Queen of England came to personally renovate the apartment in Building C. "Is it close to ours?"

"No. It's in a different part of the city." A nice part, judging by the address.

I don't say anything about timelines. I'm still in disbelief myself. I knew Will Leblanc was rich. I assumed he was powerful, like all people with money are powerful. I knew he was good at managing his company. I knew he was meticulous.

What I didn't expect is how easily he'd take over at the apartment.

I only had one goal: put everything I could into clear garbage bags. I couldn't think much beyond that. I knew how it would go. Angry apartment administrators. Another even shittier living situation for the twins. A long, long wait.

Not so, once Mr. Leblanc entered the picture.

He didn't ask people to come put the apartment back together again on an impossible deadline. He told them they'd do it. Mr. Leblanc briskly agreed to pay triple the rates to more than one of the contractors he called. I never got the impression that any of them hesitated.

Movers showed up at two o'clock. Three people to take out the bags of clothes and books and the very small collection of ragged stuffed animals the twins have managed to keep. It was loaded into the back of Mr. Leblanc's SUV in less than five minutes.

They'd just stepped out when two guys from the construction company came to survey the damage. I passed the cleaning team on the way out of the building. I bet they already have the broken plaster out of the living room.

"Is he nice?" Mia stares out the window at the city blocks rolling by.

Nice isn't the word for Will Leblanc. Yes, we're being driven to his apartment in a pristine SUV driven by a man in a suit. Yes, he's miraculously summoned people to repair the apartment.

Yes, he blackmailed me instead of calling the police.

Nice?

"He's very nice. And very busy. His work is very important to him."

"We won't get in the way," Ben says.

"Yes, we will." Mia rolls her eyes. "We're always in the way."

"You are not in the way. He invited us to stay with him, which was very nice."

The driver pulls to the curb in front of an apartment building. My pulse ticks up. This is a *building* building. There's a valet out front. I wouldn't be surprised if there were security guards inside.

"Okay. We're here. Quiet voices in the lobby, okay?"

The twins are solemn as we go inside. They have the air of people entering a museum. Or a church. Mia stares up at the ceiling and its ornamental decorations. I head in the general direction of the front desk. There are two doormen behind a shining marble counter.

One of them steps toward us before I can launch into what's surely a very awkward explanation. He wears a polite, open smile. "Ms. Anderson."

"That's me, yes. Hi."

"Mr. Leblanc asked me to bring you up as soon as you arrived. This way, please." He takes us to an elevator. When the doors are open, he steps inside with us and presses the button for Mr. Leblanc's floor. My stomach drops as we're whisked upward. What's he like at home? Angry, like he is in the office? Charming, like he was at dinner?

The elevator lets us off. The doorman leads us to a door and knocks three times. A short pause, and then it opens.

The Will Leblanc it reveals isn't the one from the office *or* the dinner. He's wearing jeans and a dark green long-sleeved shirt with the sleeves pushed up to his elbows.

He has a dish towel in one hand.

When he sees me, his face brightens. My heart skips a beat. This is the smile I wondered about at the restaurant. A real one. His eyes have never looked so blue.

"Bristol." Mr. Leblanc steps out into the hallway. "And these are your siblings?"

"This is Mia." I put my hand on the top of her head. "And Benjamin."

Mr. Leblanc offers his hand to shake. Mia, then Ben. "I'm Will Leblanc. Most people call me Will. You can, too. Do you like Benjamin or Ben?"

"Ben." Ben stares up at Mr. Leblanc like he's a god. "But some people call me Benjamin anyway."

"Those people should learn some manners. And you go by Mia?"

Mia nods, silent.

"Do you like Minecraft?" Mr. Leblanc asks.

Mia's mouth drops open. "You've heard of it?"

Mr. Leblanc laughs. "Who hasn't? What platform is your favorite?"

Ben and Mia exchange a look. "We sneak time on the school computers," Ben admits.

"My computers are better than the school computers. You won't have nearly as much lag. Come check them out. I've got graphics cards that aren't even on the market yet."

The doorman leaves, and Mr. Leblanc takes us inside. Once the door shuts, he gestures into his apartment. "Living room straight ahead. Guest room to the left. My room's on the right, along with my office. Kitchen's that way, too. A couple more rooms that aren't very interesting. The computers are in the guest room."

Mr. Leblanc's guest room is actually a guest suite. It has a giant attached bathroom and includes a sitting area. A small desk has been set up in the sitting area. Two laptops. Two chairs. Mia can't help herself. She darts over to one of the laptops.

"You already had Minecraft on here?" she says to Mr. Leblanc.

A timer beeps somewhere else in the apartment. "Make sure they work for me, okay?"

That's all the twins need to descend on the laptops. I follow Mr. Leblanc out of the bedroom and down to the kitchen.

"Please tell me you didn't buy laptops just for the twins." Except he said the graphics cards aren't even on the market yet. Which means he did more than buy them—he called in favors with tech companies. It's the kind of debt I can't begin to repay, not on top of everything else.

In the kitchen, he turns off the stove timer and opens the oven. He uses the dishcloth to take out a tray of chocolate chip cookies. Grabs a spatula. Slides them onto a cooling rack. Then the tray goes onto the stovetop.

"Do you want something to drink?" he asks.

"Mr. Leblanc."

"Will."

Shock. Pure shock. "You want me to call you that?"

"You're staying with me. In my apartment. Call me Will." He looks at me over his shoulder as he pulls open the fridge. "It was a lucky guess about Minecraft, okay? Don't worry about the computers. Those were just sitting around."

"As inventory?"

"As beta models."

"Oh my God."

"The laptops don't matter." Mr. Leblanc—*Will*—hands me a bottled Frappuccino. The kind from Starbucks that you can get at the store. Vanilla flavor. It's my favorite kind.

"Did you buy these for me?"

"Obviously. You have at least one every day in the office."

I didn't think he noticed. The break-room fridge at Summit is filled with expensive stuff like this. I've been taking advantage while I can.

My heart is warm. So warm that it spreads out all through my chest. Warm, and painfully curious. Painfully confused. How is he like this?

"Cookies?"

"There's pizza coming in an hour."

"The twins will be beside themselves. This is probably the best day of their lives."

Will smiles, this one smaller. Almost tentative. "It's the little things."

"Whoever taught you how to host kids fresh off a week of school must be very proud right now." The bottle in my hand is cold and perfect. "Was it your mom who made cookies for you growing up?"

His eyes go blank, like he's looking at nothing. Barely in the room. It's over in less time than it takes to type *Summit*. The smile is still on Will's face, but it's less open now.

"No," he says. "I saw it in a movie. But everyone knows pizza is perfect for Friday nights."

The twins play Minecraft until the pizza comes. Will spends dinner asking them which classes they like the best and how things are going on their Minecraft server. We watch a movie about a mouse who becomes a spy. They're exhausted by nine o'clock, and I tuck them into the bed in the guest bedroom. Mia's asleep before her head hits the pillow.

Will's waiting in the living room when I pad back out, hands in his pockets.

Awkwardness descends. Without the twins to focus on, it's just us. My face gets hot at the sight of him standing there. Comfortable. At home. A place I should never be. Just existing in his living room with him feels as intimate as sex.

I open my mouth to ask about sleeping arrangements when my attention catches on a swirl of color behind him. I'm walking toward it before I have any hope of getting a grip. I'm looking at an art print, that's all. A really, really good art print.

Except it's not a print. I can see brushstrokes. "Will, is this—"

"An original Van Gogh, yeah."

Yeah, like having a priceless original painting on your wall is no big deal. I'm stricken with the sudden fear that I'll spill soup on it somehow, never mind that there's no soup in sight. "You're into art?"

"My brother is a fairly famous art collector. I used to have a limited-edition print in here, but he didn't think it was up to par."

I turn around and stare at him, then cut a glance at the Van Gogh to make sure it's still there and untainted by soup. "You have a brother who just casually owns paintings like this? And hands them out?"

He smiles. "Not much about Emerson is casual."

"Tell me you don't have a third brother who's, like, a king or something."

"No. Sinclair is an investigative journalist."

"But journalists…"

"Don't worry. He's rich, too. Reward money."

"For a *hostage*?"

"For saving a prince from certain death in some crevasse in the Himalayas."

"Are you lying?"

Will's eyes twinkle. He's enjoying this. But he's careful about these details. Even now, I recognize that he's hardly told me anything. This is only the second time he's mentioned his family. "No, of course not."

"I…" *Tell me everything about you. Everything you can think of. I want to know.* I can't say any of that to Will. To my boss, who won't be my boss in a week. To the man who's blackmailing me. "Where do you want me for the night? The couch is more than fine."

He shakes his head. My heart beats faster.

"It's… not fine?"

"There's not a chance in hell you're sleeping on the couch." A brief, almost imperceptible pause. "Unless you're going to insist on it."

Unless I don't want to sleep with him. "Where else did you have in mind?"

Will crosses to me then. He puts his hand on the small of my back and guides me away from his original Van Gogh. Down a short hallway. We pass a couple of other doors before he pushes one open.

We step into his bedroom.

I don't know what I was expecting, but this…

"Oh, wow." I take a few more steps inside. The carpet feels like clouds. The shade of navy on the walls is the prettiest I've ever seen, aside from the Van Gogh in the living room. There are *details* in here. Molding on the walls. The most perfect side tables. "This is beautiful, Will."

"Do you think?"

I turn back and find him with his hands in his pockets, waiting to see if I'll take it back.

"Yes. It's like something out of a magazine, but better."

"The designer I hired was supposed to be good. I'm glad I didn't waste my money."

His whole apartment is like this. I see it now. "She was *very* good."

"Because it doesn't seem like anything I would choose?" His tone is almost playful, but his expression is guarded.

"Because it fits you so well."

The hint of a frown crosses his face, but he takes a breath. "The door on your right is the bathroom. Walk-in closet's over that way."

This bedroom has everything. A TV set into the wall across from a big bed, flawlessly made up. An ottoman at the foot. Built-in shelves.

"You can get a closer look if you're that interested, Ms. Anderson."

I've been caught staring, and the heat from my face spreads down to my chest. "I *am* interested."

"Like I said." As if I deserve privacy to snoop, Will heads into the bathroom. Water runs.

I can't help myself. The shelves have a neat arrangement of items, and I'm drawn in. A woman's watch rests on one of the higher shelves, almost above my line of sight. It's old, but clean. No dust. I don't touch it.

A polished rock.

A picture frame.

I've just lifted it off the shelf when the bathroom door opens and Will comes to stand beside me. I tilt it toward him. "Are these your brothers?"

"Couldn't you tell?"

It's obvious, on second glance. All three of them have very similar eyes. They're standing in front of a huge stone pillar in the sun. A younger Will is on the right, beaming, body turned in toward his brothers. I tap his shirt with a fingernail.

"This is you, so…"

"Emerson's in the middle. Sin's on the left."

"Was this a vacation?"

"No. Just a day in the city. We all lived here at the time."

"And now?"

"Emerson lives out toward Bishop's Landing, on the beach. Sinclair lived in LA for a few years, but he's in town now."

"Is he the oldest?" Sinclair is the only one of them with dark hair. He stands on Emerson's other side, an arm slung across his shoulders. His other hand is on Emerson's chest, like he's holding him in place. It looks very casual. Like whoever took the picture said *get together* and that's just what they did. That closeness warms my heart.

"Yes. And I'm the baby."

I don't mean to laugh, but it takes me by surprise to hear Will say it in such a dry tone. "You're at least twenty in this."

"Twenty-two."

"You're all so happy."

"It was a good day."

I scan their faces again. Will does look happy. Almost violently so. Sinclair's smiling too, but there's more in his eyes than happiness. He looks like a man who narrowly escaped a brush with death. He's relieved about something, that's for sure. Emerson looks a *lot* like Will. But the way he looks into the camera is different. Intense. It's strange, how alike they are, and how different. Emerson's smile is faint, but he looks proud.

"Where was this taken? You look like you won a prize."

Will laughs, the sound soft. "In front of the Met."

My brother is a fairly famous art collector. "Oh, that

makes total sense. Did you go with your brother to visit?"

"Yes. We walked there."

He says it like it was an accomplishment. I glance at Will to see if he's teasing. He's not. "From really far away?"

"From fifteen blocks away." Will plucks the frame out of my hands and puts it back on the shelf. The next moment, he's covering my mouth with his hand. "No more questions, Ms. Anderson."

"Bristol," I say into his palm as he steers me toward the bed.

"No more questions, Bristol."

He pulls my shirt over my head. My bra. I'm naked in a matter of seconds. Will flips back the covers and I scramble into the bed, my nerves on fire. It reminds me of turning out the light and leaping for the mattress as a kid, only I don't catch my breath once I'm away from the edge. I can't. Will's stripping his own clothes off, and it's impossible to breathe. He has muscles for days.

I wanted to see him without clothes. Wished for it. And now it's happening.

Will climbs into the bed, crawls over me, and reaches. His phone hits the bedside table while I look up at the most perfect chest I've ever seen. It's the ideal torso.

Then the lights go out.

His eyes come back into view, pale in the city light

leaking through the window.

I have no idea what's going to happen right now.

Sex in his office? That's one thing.

In his *bed?*

A shiver runs through me. Maybe now is when he'll show me the Will Leblanc that doesn't come into the office. *To be clear, I'd like to make you cry.*

He notices my shiver, the corner of his mouth turning up. I've never been so aware of a man's body, and he's barely touching me. His taut weight is balanced on his forearms so he can study my face.

"What are you afraid of?" he murmurs.

Myself. That's the real answer. Part of me wants to know what he's like in the dark, in his own home. Part of me wants to see his face at the sight of my tears.

"That I won't be able to pay you back. For this, on top of everything else."

"I told you not to worry about the laptops."

"For… letting me sleep in your bed."

Will purses his lips. I wouldn't mind making out with him forever. It's a thought I'm not supposed to have. This is about debt. This is about a two-week contract. There's no such thing as forever.

"A thousand dollars."

My heart misses a beat. "What?"

"You're paying me back whether you call me Will and sleep in my bed or not. Be good for me and spread your legs. That's good for a thousand off what you owe."

The words fill me with shame and heat. This is sex for money. A transaction. I'm a prostitute.

Will laughs, low and dark. "I felt your hips move, sweetheart. You like being a corporate whore."

What he's saying makes perfect sense. It's what I agreed to. But I feel a faint disappointment, like the first raindrops leaking through our smashed ceiling.

It's distance. That's what it is. I can sleep in his bed. I don't get to know the hidden part of him.

It's safer this way. I know that. Because the hidden part of Will Leblanc is dangerous.

I spread my legs for him, wide, accepting, and watch his pupils expand in the dark.

Two things happen at once. His hand comes down over my mouth, and his body settles over mine. He pushes himself inside me. One slow, hard thrust. It lights me up, nerve after nerve.

But nothing is more electric than Will's face.

For a split second, just as he bottoms out, his lips part. A wrinkle appears between his eyebrows. He looks like a man who's just walked in the door after surviving a long, harrowing journey, finally home.

All of his weight rests on me.

One heartbeat.

I make a sound against his palm. I don't know what I'm trying to say, or ask, or beg for.

Then he's moving, face hot with concentration. He fucks me until I'm short on breath and desperate to come. Will angles himself back, creating just enough space to slide his hand between us, and then he stares down into my eyes while he works my clit.

I come all over him, the sounds I can't stop caught in his palm.

I'm still coming when he uncovers my mouth and uses that hand to turn my head. Will leans down close to my ear. "Quiet," he orders. "Be a good corporate whore."

I know you're not supposed to sleep in your boss's bed. I know you're not supposed to let him fuck you with his hand over your mouth in exchange for a thousand dollars. I know you're not supposed to fall for him, just a little, when he forgets to treat you like a corporate whore.

Will drops his head down next to mine, his teeth grazing my shoulder. The angle of his hips sends me up toward another orgasm, but he doesn't seem to notice. He's too busy fucking me. His breath hitches when I start to come again.

But he doesn't call me a corporate whore. He whispers *fuck, Bristol.* Puts a hand on the side of my face. Pushes himself in deeper and deeper, muscles working through his own release.

No, I'm not supposed to fall for him. I'm only supposed to pay him back.

I do it anyway.

Chapter Seventeen
Will

My phone buzzes once on the bedside table.

The length of the vibration is highly specific. It's a message in the group text with my brothers. It's one of the only notifications I don't silence between midnight and five.

For a long time, when we'd drifted apart, nobody texted the group. But since Emerson met Daphne and married her, and since Sinclair has made it his mission in life to annoy the hell out of me in New York City, we've been talking.

We've been closer. The way we were in that damned photo Bristol found like she was pulled in by a laser beam.

It's a risky investment, being close to my brothers. Not one I'd usually make. One I'd usually know better than to make.

But I'm not thinking about investments when I reach

for the phone. I'm barely awake. I've been sleeping deeply. Dreamless. I snatch it up and swing my legs over the side of the bed. Cover the screen with a cupped hand. These things get brighter every year.

Emerson: *Come over*

My heart rate spikes.

Emerson texting *come over* is not a thing. His invitations are always for a reason. He'll invite us to come surf with him, or have dinner with him and Daphne, or see a new piece of art. Never like this. Never in the middle of the night.

Writing *come over* in the group text with nothing else is a desperate demand if I've ever heard one. It's the same as writing 9-1-1.

I'm not invested enough in my brothers to haul my ass out of bed and respond to their emergencies. That's what I tell myself all the way across the room and into the walk-in closet. I still believe it while I throw on boxers. Sweatpants. Hoodie. I'm being very fucking convincing when I text the night-shift valet and tell him to bring my SUV to the front of the building as fast as he can.

I'm collecting my wallet from the bedside table when the covers rustle. "Will?"

Bristol. Holy fuck, she's in my bed. She's *still* in my bed. She didn't flee to the couch after I fucked her and cleaned her up and dressed her in one of my T-shirts. She didn't go anywhere, because I tucked her into bed next to me and let her fall asleep.

It wasn't what I wanted to do. Wasn't *all* I wanted to do. But it was what a man who lives in an apartment like this would do.

"Everything's fine. Go back to sleep."

What am I saying? The only thing I can say. I can't ask her to leave. I don't want to. She and her siblings are here with me until her apartment is repaired. Bristol's here in my bed because where else is she going to sleep?

She pushes herself up from the pillow. "How come you're dressed? Are you leaving?"

"Yes."

"I can go. It's really okay, Will. You should have said—"

I climb back onto the bed, push her down into the pillows, and kiss her. I don't know what I was thinking, letting her in this far. Kissing her like this. I feel like the roof is about to cave in.

Bristol blinks up at me when I let go.

"I'm going to my brother's house. I'll be back soon."

And Bristol will still be here. She'll stay, because she doesn't have anywhere else to go.

"Is everything okay?" She's sweet. Soft. I want to stay with her, too, and that is absolutely fucking unhinged. I can't want any of this domestic bullshit.

"Nothing to worry about. Go back to sleep."

Nothing to worry about, my ass. My SUV's waiting at the curb. I force a tip into the valet's hand at top speed and gun it away from the building. Nervous. Irritated. I don't know what *come over* means. I don't know what's gone wrong. What I do know is that if Emerson could have added more details, he would have.

I dial Sin.

"Where are you?" He's breathless when he answers, like he's running.

"On my way out of the city. The hell is this about?"

"I don't know. He's been good lately."

Good, because of Daphne. Good, because our dad is back behind bars. When he got out on parole last winter, everything went to hell. Emerson just about lost his mind. It didn't help that our asshole father showed up at his house.

He should have come for me. I'd have welcomed the fight.

He never had the courage.

"This text doesn't sound good."

"No," Sinclair agrees. "Be right there."

There's no traffic to slow things down on the way to Emerson's. He lives outside the city in a huge beach house where he can store his most important pieces and stay relatively secluded from the world. It's a big step up from the first place he shut himself away in.

His front gate swings open ahead of me. A shadow moves closer to the driveway as I go through. One of the guys from Emerson's security staff. His wife's family is notorious in the city. They weren't about to let her live here without as much security as the fucking president.

None of them stop me. There were meetings about this early on. Our cars have sensors now that tell the gate to open automatically. My phone will unlock Emerson's front door when I get close enough. There's an app that can do even more.

No lights are on inside. I don't know what that means, either.

I pull up to his porch and take the stairs two at a time. No sign of Sinclair's car yet. At the door, I stop to catch my breath. Calm the hell down.

The door unlocks with a soft *click*.

I open it. Step inside. Wait for my eyes to adjust.

Emerson's place wasn't designed like mine. It's more subdued. Most of it is like a homey, eight-thousand-square-foot art gallery. It's so quiet I can hear the waves rolling on the beach.

The main feature Emerson's house has in common with mine is that it's very, *very* clean. It smells lemony. The citrus reminds me of Bristol, warm in my bed.

"Em?"

Silence.

Doesn't feel great. My pulse gets louder, thrumming

over the waves. I thought he'd be waiting in the foyer when I got here. I didn't plan on a search. I don't know where I'd begin to look. Small spaces, obviously, but there are a ton of rooms in this house.

"Where are you, motherfucker?"

I push open the door to his office. Nothing inside but moonlight. There's a dining room across the way, also empty. A tall package leans against one wall. He had a painting delivered. That's normal, at least.

Nobody in the den. Nobody in the kitchen. My footsteps feel loud as hell.

There are more rooms on the ground floor. Nothing, nothing, nothing.

The door to Emerson's biggest gallery is partially open.

I put a palm to the heavy wood and push it out of my way. Emerson's wife is an artist who loves to paint the ocean. The gallery is full of her pieces. There are several new ones, added since they got married.

I don't hear him. Don't see him.

Just silence and art. A silence that sets my teeth on edge.

I stride in, my irritation at its peak. The door begins to close behind me. "What the ever-loving *fuck*, Emerson? You—"

There's a single footstep on the wood floor.

I whip toward the sound, my brain a scramble of

Dad and *someone's out there* and *fight*.

My hand comes up in a fist.

Emerson's faster.

He comes out of nowhere, his fists colliding with my chest. The last shred of my civilized brain, the one not choking on adrenaline and old memories, notes that it's not a hit. It's a grab. He's got my sweatshirt in a hard grip. I shove against it on instinct. Against him, backing us up a few feet. Stay ready to punch him.

Older, a small voice whispers. *Dangerous*.

The force of his hold on my sweatshirt backs this up, and for a heartbeat I'm not Will Leblanc, billionaire entrepreneur and underground boxer. I'm *Will, if you fucking breathe wrong, you're never coming outside again. I heard that, you little bastard. I'll make you wish you were dead.*

Except it's not my father with my shirt in his fists. It's my brother.

It's basically my own face looking back at me, except his expression is cold and distant and blank. It's the face I might have had if our childhood turned me into a person instead of a monster. Make no mistake, he's fucked up. But he's fucked up in a human way. Not like me.

His eyes say he might as well be on another planet. Lost in the galleries he sees in his head. It's only the tremble in Emerson's fists that gives any indication he's still here.

This is *definitely* not good.

"Emerson." I pull the punch. Push at him instead. "*Em.*"

He shakes his head, the motion so slight it's practically nothing. *No.* That's all I get.

"Listen. Whatever it is, it's going to be okay. I'll wait with—"

Emerson hauls me in closer. "No. It's. Not. I want it to *stop.*"

He sounds like he's suffocating. Like he might kill me for making the suggestion. "Jesus, Em. Just—"

The door to the gallery swings open. It doesn't make any noise, but Sinclair does. "Let go of him."

For a single instant, I think Sin's talking to me. Coming to *me.* Good. I'm finally the one he'll tackle.

But...no. I'm not the one holding on. I'm not the one with any kind of problem to be solved.

"Emerson. Let go." Sinclair doesn't give Em any time to release his grip. He just drags him away from me, turns him sideways, and throws his arms around him in a half-tackle, half-hug.

Emerson sucks in a breath and pushes hard at Sinclair, who doubles down on the hug. I shake out my clothes and try to look less like a useless bastard. A jealous bastard.

Jealous of what? Not Emerson. He's struggling to

breathe. His chest is moving too fast. Too shallow. Every breath sounds pinched, like he's taking it through a straw. Concentration darkens his face. Frustration. His hands go up and hook around Sin's forearm. It looks like he's trying to pull Sin's arm away, but he's not. He's pushing it toward him with more force. I should have done this already. Should have batted his fists away from my sweatshirt and done the only thing that ever helps.

"Can't get it to stop," Emerson says.

Fresh guilt constricts my throat. It hurts more to see now that he's had a stretch of good months. He even made it through his wedding. Through the weeks of intense planning and practice to the ceremony and reception. But what our childhood did to his mind is always waiting for a chance to fuck him up again. I'm responsible for it as much as our bastard of a father.

"It's all right, Em." Sin catches my eye. His expression is calm, like he's not giving a bone-crushing hug to a man who's going to drown with his head fully above water. "You okay?"

"I'm fine."

I've been fine for a long, long time.

"If it doesn't stop, we'll wait with you," Sinclair announces to Emerson. There's no way to head off what's already happening. Is there? "Where's Daphne?"

Her absence punches dread into my gut. It's bad fucking news if Emerson's hiding it from his wife. He doesn't hide anything from her.

It's especially bad if he's spiraling here. Emerson almost never has panic attacks inside his house. It's when he leaves that things get tenuous.

Emerson grits his teeth. Forces a deeper breath. "Asleep."

Sinclair waits a few beats. Readjusts his grip around Emerson's shoulders.

My mind replays other, older memories.

Sin, tackling Emerson away from a cracked curb, their bodies going down hard on concrete while traffic went by at forty miles an hour. Sin, blocking the front door of a crumbling split-level while Emerson fought him with everything he had. A surprising amount, given how long he'd been locked in the closet. *You can't go out there, Em. I know. I know.* Sin, both palms on Emerson's chest, pushing him into the brick facade of a building one and a half blocks from the apartment we lived in after we left home. *I can't do this.* Emerson's voice, agonized. *I can't. I'm done. I can't.*

"Did she paint today?" Sin's casual about the question, like Emerson's not fighting. He's not trying to get free. He's trying to stop the full-body tremors that go along with the worst of his panic.

It looks more painful than getting punched in the face.

Emerson doesn't answer. What I can see of his expression has gone absent. His body claws for air. His mind is somewhere else.

"I noticed the new piece, by the way. Another great one. I see why you didn't sell it. I especially like what she's done with the light on the water. Makes you wonder if it's dawn or dusk." I turn my head and find that Sin's talking about the painting on the wall behind me, just visible in the moonlight. Something real to use as an anchor. A waypoint out of the imagined galleries Emerson sometimes disappears into during panic attacks. I wonder if Sin learned this trick from Daphne, or if I'm the only one who didn't know. "It's okay, Em. Completely safe. You can come back if you want."

Sin holds tighter. Waits some more. Waits fucking forever.

I'm about to ask him whether he thinks this will get worse when Emerson's grip on Sin's arm loosens. Some of the tension in his shoulders releases. Thank fuck. It's almost over. Or Sinclair actually managed to help him hold it off.

"Okay." Emerson gasps a breath. "Okay. Fuck."

Sin takes him over to the sitting area in the center of the room. He nods at one of the chairs, and I take it. Then he pushes Emerson onto the couch and takes the spot next to him, one hand on his shoulder.

Emerson sits at the edge of the cushions, his hands over his face. They're still trembling. I've seen him this way lots of times. Not as much as Sin, though.

"I'm sorry," Emerson says to the room at large. "It's late."

"Is Daphne okay?" Sin asks.

I hold my breath. My brother is obsessed with his wife. So obsessed that he kidnapped her like an unhinged asshole.

Who are you to judge? says that voice. *You're blackmailing Bristol.*

It's not the same thing.

Daphne's just as obsessed with Emerson. That she's not here is unsettling to say the least. She's always there for him.

If anything ever happened to her, we'd lose him.

Emerson pulls his hands down. He's got his gallery expression on now. Careful. Neutral. But he's too pale in the moonlight.

"She's pregnant."

He braces himself, and all that careful neutrality drops away. He's terrified. His eyes go from me to Sin and back again. Fuck. He's waiting for us to confirm that this is, in fact, a disaster.

Sinclair blinks, surprised, and then he slaps Emerson lightly on the shoulder. "Congratulations, Em."

Emerson stares. "What?"

"Your wife is pregnant. That's a good thing."

"You've fucking lost it." Emerson lets out a disbelieving laugh and holds his hands up in front of him. They're still shaking. "Look at me."

Sinclair looks back. "So?"

"So what if I can't do it?"

"Do what?"

"Be a father, Sin." Emerson's sharp. Struggling for control. "I can't let her see me like this. Daphne can't know that this is what happened when she told me. You can't tell her. Ever."

He looks away, into nothing, and I see the effort this conversation is taking.

"What are you afraid of?" I meant to keep my mouth shut. Too late.

Emerson meets my eyes. "What if she can't trust me?"

To be alone with the baby. To not panic. To keep his own child safe.

He's really asking, *what if I can't trust myself?*

Sinclair rubs at his shoulder. "Daphne already knows everything about you. She loves you. And I bet she's so excited."

"She's over the fucking moon." Emerson's absolutely miserable. I understand why he didn't want her to see this. He thinks it would break her heart.

If Bristol stays at my apartment much longer, she'll see *me*. Shame burns hot under my clothes. All the things I've paid for won't hide the truth from her. Even telling her that a fuck in my bed is worth a thousand dollars won't be enough. She could be awake even now, lying there in the dark, picking it apart. I can hear her soft, disappointed murmur. *I knew it wasn't real.*

"It's going to be different." Sinclair waits until Em is looking at him to continue. "It's not going to be like it was with Dad. You're not like that. And you're not by yourself anymore."

It feels like a knife slipping into my gut. Such a simple phrase. *You're not like that.* Of course Emerson's not like Dad. He thought he was because he kidnapped Daphne. That's bullshit. He worships her. And she went to pieces without him.

I'm the one who's like Dad.

I'm the violent fuck who attends underground boxing matches because he can't get enough of fists and faces. Heat spreads across the back of my neck. All my money, all my success, and I'm still the same.

"Will," Sinclair prompts.

Emerson's looking at me. Searching. He's done that for as long as I can remember. Looked at people's faces for longer than anyone else. I'm supposed to say something, clearly. The last part of Sin's sentence catches up.

"Yeah. We're here, too. And Daphne's family."

We're here, but I shouldn't be. Not now, and not when his baby is born. A better person would tell the truth.

I can't do it.

"We'll figure it out." Sinclair gives an easy shrug. "Honestly, Em. There's nobody better at taking care of Daphne than you. It'll be the same for the baby. But we can be here whenever you need us."

Emerson glances between the two of us again. "It's a lot to ask."

"I don't keep score," Sin says.

"You should." Em rubs a hand over his face. "You know that."

Because he owes Sinclair his life. Our older brother has waited Emerson out through panic attacks much worse than this one. Dragged him away from speeding traffic and his most dangerous impulses many, many times.

"Too much work." Sin leans back on the couch. "Em."

Emerson looks at him. He's tired. Pale. Hopeful.

"It's great news. We're fucking thrilled for you."

Okay. That's what Emerson means to say, but no sound comes out. A tentative smile flashes over his face.

"You got any good news, Will?" Sinclair asks.

"I have a contract to merge with Hughes Financial Services." It comes out flat and irritated. *Don't take the deal unless you're ready to take orders.* That'll be the day.

Emerson's eyebrows go up. He clears his throat, still

obviously shaken. "Is it a hostile takeover?"

"No. They're giving me a superyacht."

Sinclair considers me. "Not the superyacht you wanted?"

"The yacht's fine."

It's all the rest of this shit that's not. I want Bristol. I want to be in bed with Bristol right now.

I feel no satisfaction when I think about the contract. About *taking orders* from Finn Hughes. But when I think about her?

Yes.

That cannot be what she represents. It's not possible. Women always walk out the door. My mother is a prime example.

And me? I shouldn't be in the same city as Bristol, much less the same bedroom.

"Was Dad less of an asshole before Mom left?"

Sin's eyebrows draw together. "He was always a prick."

"But was he worse after she was gone?"

I know that she probably left because he was a monster, but I can't help thinking that it was the other way around. That Dad became who he was because she left. And we were the ones who suffered for it.

"I can't say for sure." Sinclair shifts forward, watching me. "Did it seem that way to you?"

"Seemed like you shouldn't have come back."

He scoffs, tone light. "Wasn't going to leave my brothers."

But Sinclair *did* leave. He was the only one who had a chance to leave. Our mother took him with her. The only reason he came back to hell is because of us.

"Not until later, you mean."

Sin nods, accepting what I've said. "Not until I thought we were doing okay. I'm not saying it was the right call."

"It was."

A beat. "I don't know if I believe you, Will."

"Can't change anything now."

It's not true. Look at Emerson. *He* changed. He texted us in the middle of the night. Before, he'd have suffered until morning.

And he's worried about having a baby with Daphne. Why?

I'm the one who hasn't changed. I'm a monster, just like our dad, otherwise I wouldn't need to work so hard to prove otherwise. I wouldn't need expensive suits and a designer for my apartment and all my rules at work. I would never have touched Bristol.

I should leave her alone. Leave her whole family alone. They're in trouble, and that's all I am—trouble.

It's best for us if we stick to our outlets. Sinclair has BASE jumping. Emerson has art. And I have violence.

That's all I'll ever have.

Chapter Eighteen
Bristol

THE ALARM ON my phone rings early, and I feel...
Great.
Rested.
Will's mattress probably had something to do with it.

He sits up as soon as I do and runs his hands over his hair. Then he's padding to the bathroom, leaving me behind. He re-emerges a few minutes later.

Add this to the list of things I know about Will LeBlanc: the way he looks in sleep pants and a thin T-shirt. Broad shoulders. Full chest. Tight abs.

"When did you get back last night? I felt you, I think." I can't help smiling, but his smile is reserved. Businesslike. His eyes slip down over my body in the sheets, but they come up quickly.

Too quickly.

"Late."

"Is everything all right?"

"Yes. Everything's fine."

Fine, but he doesn't crawl back into bed with me. He doesn't kiss me.

Something happened.

Or else Will Leblanc really can't exist in the world without coffee.

I throw on clothes and follow him to the kitchen, where he makes it using the same beans he uses in the office.

A few more items on the list: the faint, masculine smell of him when he first wakes up. The way he stands at the window of his apartment, mug in hand, pensive and still as the first rays of sun break through the skyscrapers. The way he wears worn-in, soft clothes on the weekend, the opposite of his suits.

Coffee doesn't improve the distance between us.

He's great with the twins. Patient. Easygoing. I hear them all laughing about Minecraft after lunch.

But he's pulled away from me. I'm sure of it by Saturday night.

"I really don't mind sleeping on the couch," I tell him, an hour after the twins have fallen asleep.

"I mind."

He's just as quiet when we're under the covers together.

I lie carefully on the pillow. This is what they mean when they say *paralyzed by confusion*. I want to roll over and make out with Will Leblanc, but he doesn't seem to want that. Last night feels like a dream.

"Will?"

"Yeah?"

He's relaxed, but I get the feeling it's mostly for show. I close my eyes and focus. When I do, I can feel that he's breathing a bit faster. And the energy that I thought was cold and distant and professional is…

Tension. The image of an athlete at a starting line, waiting for a gun to fire, pops into my mind. An athlete that looks like Will, with his height and his muscles and the bruise that's faded from his cheek.

"What's wrong?"

He rolls over. From the sound of his voice, he's on his back. "Nothing's wrong."

"You're not a great liar, you know."

Will huffs a bitter laugh. "Nothing is wrong, Bristol. Everything is just how it's supposed to be."

That's it.

I'm simply not the kind of woman who just lies in bed, fretting. Not when I could be doing something.

I push myself away from the pillow, crawl across the bed, and straddle him. "Pretend," I order to the dim light caught in his blue eyes.

Will's hands glide over my hips. He doesn't push me away. "What the hell are you talking about, Ms. Anderson?"

"I'm in your bed with you. It's *Bristol*. And none of this is supposed to be happening." I feel a pang at saying the words, like they're a lie. Like this isn't fate. "I wasn't supposed to steal. You weren't supposed to blackmail me. Letting me stay with you like this is obviously against the rules. But yesterday…"

"What about yesterday?" Will murmurs, his eyes tracing down my body.

"Yesterday you baked cookies and ordered pizza—"

He's solid underneath me. Strong. I'm simultaneously desperate to sink into him and desperate to make time slow down.

"And then I covered your pretty mouth with my hand and fucked you senseless," he points out.

"This is temporary." I lean down and nip the side of his neck. Will's hands flex, tensing around my hips. It pushes me down, the heat between my legs brushing against where he's hard. "We don't have that much time. Can you just pretend it's yesterday? Can you just—"

His hands thread around the back of my neck, and Will pulls me into a hard kiss. I taste the tension on him. The endless loop of his thoughts.

And then they short out into the pleasure-pain of his teeth at my bottom lip and the sudden adrenaline of the single movement he uses to roll us over.

Will's over me in the dark, his lips at the side of my neck, at my ear. "Would I just pretend to be someone else? Just for you, Bristol?"

"Not someone else."

He hooks his fingertips in the waistband of my panties and pulls them off. My shirt goes next. "Who, then?"

"You were happy." Will's stripping his own clothes off now. It's dark in the bedroom. Too dark to see the fine details of his body. That doesn't matter, because he shifts over me and I can feel every one of them. "Pretend everything's right. Pretend I'm staying, because—"

His hand comes down over my mouth.

I must be imagining the tremble in it.

"You're right," he murmurs into my ear as he nudges his tip inside me. "I *should* fuck you senseless again. I liked you that way, all pink and warm and filthy with my cum. Spread your thighs, sweetheart. Earn another thousand dollars. Pretend you're never leaving."

✧ ✧ ✧

I DON'T GET to pretend very long, because the apartment is done by Sunday afternoon.

Not just repaired—completely rebuilt.

The people Will hired didn't just fix the roof and repair the plaster. They tore out the drywall and replaced it. Then they repainted it—not the tired white that had been there before. Instead it's a comfortable mauve in the living room, a soothing greige in the bedrooms. They tore up the thin carpet, leveled the floors, and replaced it with gorgeous wood planks.

All the thrift-store bed frames have been replaced with brand new ones.

Not only that, but we rode up in the elevator.

No more sign hanging from its chain. No more dusty, closed doors. He had that fixed, too.

I can't believe it.

I keep walking from one room to the next, then stepping into the hall to make sure this is really ours.

"Bristol," Ben calls from the bedroom. "Are you sure he didn't make a mistake?"

"I'm sure."

The twins have been asking that question since we walked in fifteen minutes ago.

Will had his driver drop us off with all our things. All of it was packed into new luggage. No garbage bags.

I'm torn, because I want him to be here with me.

And if he *had* come, I'd have made a fool of myself. Because I don't have the words to thank him for this.

From my dad's remodeled bedroom, I dial the landlord. This is the part I've been dreading. Explaining how I, Bristol Anderson, pulled this off.

He answers with a chipper *what can I do for you?*

"This is Bristol Anderson, subleasing apartment three-oh-six. I wanted to let you know that—"

"Oh, I've got all the information right here. Are you all moved in again?"

"Yes?" I clear my throat. "I mean, yes. We are. But I wasn't sure if the paint colors—"

"It's all fine," he says. "Everything's taken care of."

This from the man who forbade us from hanging so much as a Post-it note on the walls. He objected to the paper-mache wreaths my brother and sister made for the fourth of July.

He's complained about the magnets on our refrigerator, for God's sake.

"Thank you," I tell him. "Thank you so much."

Those are words for the wrong person.

Not one inch of the apartment has been left untouched. I wander back into the kitchen, which is a miniature version of Will's. I don't think we've ever lived in a place with a new oven.

It takes my breath away.

I don't want to imagine how much Will paid the landlord to be that satisfied. I don't want to imagine how much all this cost. And for it to be done in two days?

He's added a fortune to the invisible tally sheet of my debt.

I owe him more than two weeks. *Much* more.

And the foolish part of me wants it to last.

It can't. I know that. I know better than to trust powerful men. Especially powerful men who show up to work with bruises on their faces and stalk away from me on the street.

After a weekend in his apartment, I know Will Leblanc isn't who he pretends to be in the office. An old instinct is certain that he's a dangerous man.

The good, warm feelings from the time I spent in his bed don't change it.

I *know* better, and I still want his secrets. I still want access to all the things he hides behind his suits and his money.

The question is, how much more am I willing to pay?

Chapter Nineteen
Bristol

I DON'T KNOW who I'll meet at the office on Monday morning. It won't be the Will from Friday night. That's the only version of him I can rule out.

The pressure around my heart grows on the way into the office.

I know something was bothering him on Saturday. The fact that he wouldn't tell me what it was felt like coming home to find an eviction notice on the door. The locks changed.

What we have together, as wrong as it is, feels real. Right up until the moment my fingertips meet a pane of glass, and I discover I'm in a blackmail maze. The only exit is the end of my temp job, and that's not enough time to—

To what? Get him to tell me everything? He's not going to.

I tap my foot on the elevator, impatient with everything.

I have five days left at Summit. Five days left to pay Will back.

Now I owe him twice as much, and that's a conservative estimate.

Plus, it's going to bother me forever if I never learn anything else about him. This past weekend was a tease. A fifteen-second preview of an epic movie series.

By the time the elevator slows to a stop, I've made up my mind. I'm just going to ask him about it. Insist on an answer. I don't have unlimited time to convince him to tell me.

I never have unlimited time. That's just not what life with my dad is like. The temp agency is actually a perfect fit, because he never stays in one place for long. My entire life is a temp job, when you think about it.

The elevator doors open, and I stride out, determined.

I flash a smile at the receptionist.

She doesn't smile back. Instead, she holds up her hand. "Bristol. Mr. Leblanc is waiting for you in the conference room?"

Shit. "He is?"

"He expects you there as soon as you arrive."

"Okay. Thanks."

My blood feels cool and anxious now. My clothes have never felt cheaper. Even my shoes seem off-balance.

He didn't tell me there was an early meeting.

I rush through the office, abandon my purse at my desk, and grab the first notebook and pen that come to hand.

Then I peek into Will's office, half-hoping the receptionist is wrong.

He's not there.

I want to run to the conference room, but I don't. I choose my steps carefully. I take even, steady breaths.

I'm steps away from the conference room door when laughter spills out into the hall.

The laughter of at least three men.

Will's words ring in my ears. *You'd service every man in the conference room.*

I want to believe he wasn't serious, but he followed through on blackmail. He followed through on fucking me in his office in exchange for the money I stole.

My heart feels like bare tires on a shitty stretch of highway. It won't stop rattling.

He's waiting for me.

I take the final steps to the conference room door on shaky knees and cross the threshold before I lose my nerve. "Good morning, Mr. Leblanc."

Will sits at the head of the conference table.

One glance at his face, and I know who he is.

The volatile, demanding boss from my very first day. Impatience comes off him like a heat mirage. It looks like water on the road. Like you'll eventually drive into something cool and clear.

Will's company space might be cool and corporate, but he's not.

He's only pretending.

His apartment, his office…they offer context, and people accept him as part of it. They never see past.

There are three other men at the table with him, and they're all looking at me.

None of them looks at me like Will. His eyes scan my entire body, head to toe, and I flush wherever his gaze lands. I was just naked in his bed on Saturday night. It seems like decades ago.

Or like it never happened at all.

"Now that you're here, we'll need some water, Bristol."

I force my knees not to give out. Shame burns across my cheeks. I'm not sure whether I'm more relieved or disappointed in the order.

I don't want to have sex with any of the men sitting around the conference table. Not at all.

But I *do* want to do something hot and illicit with Will.

Anything to be as close as we were in his bed.

Anything to take advantage of the last week we have.

"I'll be right back with that."

The break room, with its kitchen and dishware, isn't

far away. I get out the small tray and the heavy water glasses. A slim container of ice. A pitcher of water. My hands don't shake at all on the way back.

I'm pretty proud of that.

In the conference room, I move around the table. The men continue their meeting as I put out the glasses. Tip ice into each one. A third round with the water.

I feel Will watching every time I bend down to pour.

He gives it a minute after I'm finished. The conversation volleys. *Contract terms* and *yes, that's easy enough to change* and *what would you think about...* fly across the table.

There's a lull. A slight pause. A little dip.

Will looks at his watch. "We'll break for about twenty minutes. I need to finalize my schedule for the afternoon."

"Perfect." One of the men laughs. "I missed breakfast this morning."

"My receptionist put out a tray of fruit and pastries in the lounge."

They're very excited about the pastries.

Will sees them out, then closes the door behind him. When he turns around again, the professional expression has disappeared from his face.

I feel a bolt of fear, then a wash of heat. I can't name his expression. Anger, I think. More. At me? At the meeting?

Will stalks around the table, a step away from crowding me. "Lie down."

I steel myself. "I was going to talk to you. I know something was up on Saturday, and I wanted to—"

"You're not finished paying me back. Lie. Down."

The weekend was a dream, then. It was nothing.

My body betrays me. It finds his heated, angry demands pretty hot.

A deep flush heats my cheeks. "On the table or on the floor?"

"The table." Will points. I see exactly where I'm supposed to lay.

Conference tables aren't made to spread out on. It's an awkward climb. I let my feet dangle over the edge, toward Will, and ease myself back.

Will narrows his eyes. "Pull up your skirt."

This isn't right. This isn't the way he was. "Are you okay?"

"I'm perfectly well, Ms. Anderson," he snaps. "Your skirt."

I yank at it, feeling slightly desperate. When my panties are exposed, Will steps in. He hooks his fingertips in the waistband and pulls them down.

All the way down.

One of my heels catches on them as he tugs them off and drops them to the conference room carpet.

"Show me what I bought, Bristol."

I know he means that I should spread my legs. What's the most wrong about the situation is how much I want to. I don't know what happened to Will between the time I left his apartment and this morning.

I don't know if it matters.

"Did something happen to you?"

He laughs, short and cruel. "This isn't about me, sweetheart. Did you get confused over the weekend and convince yourself that I'm your boyfriend?"

That one hurts. A stab wound to the heart. "No."

I spread my legs.

He makes a low sound at the sight of me. "I could smell you while you were pouring water for all those motherfuckers. I could smell how much you wanted to be fucked."

My voice trembles. "I barely noticed them. All I could think about was you."

"Did you think I was going to make you suck them off?"

"I thought you might."

Will pulls a chair up and sits between my legs. His hands on my thighs make me shiver. He pushes them open wider. I feel the stretch in my muscles. "Maybe I should call them back in here and show them how wet my secretary gets. Did you *want* me to make you suck them off, Ms. Anderson?"

I stare at the ceiling, burning with shame and hurt

and confusion. "It's not really about what I want, is it?"

"No. Would you have done it?"

"I would do whatever you said." *Because you made my siblings happy. Because you fixed my apartment. Because of the way you curl close to me when you're asleep.*

"That's right. Because if you don't, you'll get arrested, and then you'll be trapped. All locked in."

That's the second time he's mentioned being *locked in*. Not *locked up*. It gives me pause.

I would do whatever you said.

The truth spills out of me. I should *not* tell him this. Not with his hands on my thighs and his breath on a very sensitive place. "Because I can't stop thinking about you. I'm worried about you."

"You should be worried about yourself. You owe me quite a bit of money."

"I wish I owed you even more money. I wish this wasn't only two weeks."

A low laugh. Will licks me. Firm. Possessive. "That's sweet."

He licks me again, and I gasp. "Why? Why wouldn't I want you? I thought—"

"You thought fixing your apartment was proof that I'm a nice man. That I'm interested in you. That I care about you. I don't, Bristol."

"That's not—"

I don't get the chance to say *true,* because Will buries

his face between my legs. It's hot, forbidden pleasure. The conference table's hard underneath me. In less than twenty minutes, those men will file back in to talk about money.

I'm squirming in Will's grip when he stands up, the heat of him gone in a heartbeat.

"No," I whisper.

Will replaces his tongue with two fingers, pushing them in deep. So deep it hurts. I try to fuck them in spite of myself.

"Tell me about the postcard in your bedroom," he demands.

"I thought you weren't interested in me."

He pumps his fingers in and out, then stops. Holds still. It's mean. "This is a question of fairness. You spent the weekend in my apartment, going through all my things. Or did you want to be in debt for that, too? You're indebted. You have to do anything I demand, even answer my questions."

It was one picture. That's all I looked at. But it must have meant something.

"The postcard," he orders.

Somehow this feels more personal than sex. More intimate than his tongue on my clit. It makes me shiver with forced vulnerability. "It was another vacation spot. A beautiful beach."

"Why are you so obsessed with the beach, Bristol?"

"Because—" He hooks his fingers, and I almost die right there on the conference table. "Because my mom told me a story about a beach vacation she took. She was in college. Before—before I was born. And she loved it. She bought a postcard there—" His fingers are too skilled. They make me stutter and gasp. "—and she kept it for a long time. We were supposed to go together, but we didn't."

"Why?"

"Because…"

"Give me what I want, Ms. Anderson."

"Because she died."

The words feel like a shout. His fingers have gone still again, and I can't think.

"When did she die?" His voice sounds a little softer. Not quite gentle, but not angry, either. There's a shared sadness. Reciprocal, like he knows. But he's never said a word about his mother.

And the one time I mentioned her—

"Tell me."

"When I was ten. We left Arizona a couple years after that, when the twins were…" I try to do the math. It's harder than I thought at a moment like this. "They were about two."

"For where?"

"I don't remember." There were crying toddlers and empty gas tanks and cheap hotels. Apartments that seemed to fall apart around us. The next big thing was always just around the corner. "We went east. And kept going."

Will slides his fingers out of me, and I bite back a wail. I just want contact with him. I just want to come. I just want to stop talking about all of this. What good will it do?

I hear his zipper.

Then his big palms spread me another inch wider, and his tip presses against me.

"Keep talking. Keep talking while I fuck you like the corporate whore you are."

One tear slides down my cheek. He's not hurting me. I *want* this. But it doesn't make sense. If he doesn't care to know, why make me tell him these things? Why make it so good?

"Will."

"It's Mr. Leblanc when we're in the office. Mr. Leblanc when I'm fucking you over the conference table. Mr. Leblanc when I'm blackmailing you. Now tell me what happened next."

"We crossed the country while my dad looked for work."

Will pushes himself inside me, slow and relentless. The size of him steals my breath. "He didn't find any work, did he? He didn't want regular work. He wanted to steal from people. Like you."

"Yes, he—" No more room. Will bottoms out with a shiver. His teeth click together, but his eyes stay on mine. It's a cold, distant blue. "We would leave town before they started to catch on. Or after they came to beat him up."

"And what did *you* do?"

"Went to school. Took care of the twins. Tried to keep things packed up for when—" He's chosen his rhythm now. Harder strokes than I expected but it feels so good. The pad of his thumb teases at my clit. "For when we'd have to leave again."

"Were you alone, Ms. Anderson? You didn't have a big brother to protect you?"

It's bitter, when he says it like that, but I can't understand. The photo he keeps on his shelf is a happy one. Then again, maybe I can't think because I'm being fucked on a conference table.

"My brother is older." His thumb adds real pressure, and I feel myself clench around him. Will lets out a sharp breath. "He joined the military when he was eighteen. He wasn't there."

"You took care of yourself."

"Me. The twins. My dad. That's all I've done. I thought—" Pleasure builds. He's going to make me come on his cock, spread out like a corporate whore on a conference table.

"You thought what, Ms. Anderson?"

"I thought I could go to school when we finally got here." A wild laugh. "There's no more country after this. I thought we'd finally get to stay."

Will's eyes narrow, and he circles my clit with his thumb, winding me up fast and hard. The orgasm catches me by surprise. It's fast and intense, and before it's peaked, Will hauls me off the table, still impaled on him.

My back meets the conference room wall, and his hand is under my chin. I close my lips against the sounds I can't help making. Will fucks me standing up, his face blurry through the pleasure haze.

"Is that what you thought? You thought you'd get to steal a little money from me and spend the rest of your time on your knees under my desk? Is that what you wanted all along?"

I can hardly get enough air to speak. "If you let me stay—"

"If I let you stay." His eyes fall to my lips. My arms over his shoulders are nothing. I could let go, and he'd keep me upright. Keep fucking me. "I'm beginning to think that was your goal the entire time. Offer me your sweet pussy and your tits and your throat and bleed me dry."

"Mr. Leblanc—"

"How long would it have taken you to run the con to the end, Bristol? A month? A year? What would you let me do to you before you walked away?"

"I don't want to go."

"Not even if I chained you to the corner of my desk and used you for bonuses? Not even if I gave you what you deserved for stealing fifty thousand dollars?"

"*No.*"

Will pulses inside me. Shoves me harder against the wall. Angles his body so there's contact with my clit. I should not come during this conversation. Should refuse.

But the words don't match the expression on his face.

Gravity's making it impossible to refuse. Feels too good. Too good—

Will leans in when I start to come. "That's what kind of person I am, Ms. Anderson. You'd get more than you bargained for. Your con didn't work. You're not staying."

His hands say something else. They hold me firmly in place while he covers my mouth with his and comes. Will's body is all-in on the release. Every muscle pins me to the wall until he's good and finished.

At the end, he puts his head down on my shoulder. Just for a moment.

Then I'm on my feet. He pulls my skirt back into place. Rearranges his clothes. Turns away. "Go back to your desk."

"Will."

He bends, picking up my panties from the conference room floor.

"Mr. Leblanc. I—I need those."

He puts them into his pocket, a mean glint in his eyes. "You can pick them up at the end of the day."

"I—"

"Now, Bristol, or you'll serve lunch with your skirt around your waist."

I walk into the hallway, feeling the brush of a cool, air-conditioned breeze on my bare pussy.

Chapter Twenty
Will

THERE'S A LIMIT to how many times I can fight at the warehouses by the city docks every month.

The non-sanctioned fights only happen once a week. That's the agreement with the cops. There are fewer rules and more gambling, and any fucked-up asshole can get into the ring so long as nobody dies.

I've kept it to a minimum since I started Summit. Once or twice a month. I was here, what, nine days ago?

I should be fine.

And I will be, once I've had a chance to fight.

It's Bristol, that's all. Bristol and her concern and her sweetness and her two-week contract. It's Bristol and my goddamn brothers and how Emerson of all people is going to end up with everything while I end up with a superyacht and stock options. Makes my blood feel sharp and out of place.

I push open the corrugated-metal door and shoulder

my way into a restless crowd.

"—the rest of the crew out of this hellhole," a guy says. Blond. Scar on his face. "Jason's two minutes from making a challenge."

A dark-haired man laughs. It's the biggest laugh I've ever heard. It sounds like deep water and forty-foot waves. "I'm wounded, Nicholas. You think I've gone too soft to drag that kid out of here myself?"

"I think your wife will murder you if you let Jason go up against him."

I work my way closer to the ring, and—ha. That's what they're talking about.

A mountain of a man leans against the ropes, looking amused as hell. He's up there because he won the last match. He'll stay up there until he quits, or until someone beats him.

Perfect.

Nobody else came here prepared for what this is. You can prepare for your opponent. Can't trust some fancy bracket to keep you safe. There are no weight classes at these events. There's only win or lose.

I shove some people out of my way. Their faces are red with impatience. Everybody's crowded together, shouting. They want action. If nobody gets into the ring and gives it to them, they'll make their own entertainment.

The guys who take a cut from this won't be happy if

it gets out of control. Cops won't be happy, either.

There's a folding table at the side of the ring, and that's where I go. Kid named Charles sits on the table, eyeing the crowd. Old Max is next to him. They're in charge of the bets and entries. A few other people hang close, ready with tape and ice packs and bandages.

"I want in," I tell Charles.

"Name?" he says. He knows my name by now, the little prick.

"No." Hank, the guy who's in charge of the ring, puts a hand on my shoulder. "Wait until he leaves."

I take another look at the guy in the ring. He's massive. A Mack Truck.

I work out. I surf. He's easily three times my size. "Is there a waiting list I don't know about?"

"He's beat three guys in a row. Won't get out of the ring."

I want to fight. Need it. It's the only thing that will beat the savagery out of me. The only thing that will keep Bristol Anderson safe from me.

"You're going to have a riot on your hands if you don't get somebody up there. Put me in."

Charles pipes up from the table. "You could die, White Collar. Your odds are that bad. And if you die, that means a police inquiry. We can't jeopardize the fights, even for you."

What is he, twelve? I don't care if there's a police

inquiry. I don't care if I die.

"Put me in the ring."

Hank rubs a hand over the back of his neck, then sighs. "Fine. But if the bones in your hand shatter into a thousand pieces and you can't click your mouse for the rest of your life, don't come crying to me."

I turn back to Charles, who's surprised but trying to hide it. "Name," he says again.

"Will Leblanc."

Will, if you fucking breathe wrong, you're never coming outside again.

Charles writes my name down on one side of his sheet. Hank was telling the truth. Three others are above mine, all crossed out with the times of the matches written next to them.

"You're up." Charles puts his pen into the notebook and flips it closed. "Maybe say a prayer or something."

I roll my eyes at both of them and head to the girl with the tape. *White Collar.* I wore jeans, for fuck's sake. I wore a T-shirt.

A few familiar faces press closer to the ring as I climb up and in, flexing my hands, getting a feel for the tape. They're other regulars. I've trained with a couple of them before.

"Will," one of them calls. "You sure about this?"

I give him a big, cocky grin. "Can't back out now."

"Yes, you can, asshole."

The look in his eyes says I probably should back out, but I'm not going to.

I don't deserve a fancy-ass office and an overflowing bank account. I don't deserve a superyacht. I deserve *this.*

I heard that, you little bastard.

My opponent looks even bigger from inside the ring.

The ref glances at me, glances at the other guy, and frowns.

I'm known as a fairly decent boxer. I regularly win rounds on nights like these.

The mountain pushes himself away from the ropes and cracks his knuckles. Every vein in my body is strung through with adrenaline and supersaturated oxygen.

This isn't a boxing match. This is a suicide mission.

I'll make you wish you were dead.

Everybody else is happy, anyway. Crowd noise drowns out my heartbeat. The ref rushes in.

The bell rings.

Mountain Man is huge, and he's not particularly fast. He comes in easy and swipes at me with one giant hand.

I see it coming from a mile away. Plenty of time to duck, which I do. A laugh rolls over the crowd. I give them a smile, keeping my eyes on the danger.

The laugh is good for me. It gets them on my side.

It also fucks me over a little bit, because Mountain Man doesn't like it. He hops back a step, face going red.

They were cheering for him before. Waiting to see

how many people he'd knock out. Now that he's refused to leave the ring, the crowd wants an underdog.

He charges me again, faster. More seriously. He *can* move his hands at a decent speed when he wants to. A blow grazes my cheek. I use the moment to drive my fist into his gut.

The impact sends pain through my knuckles, all the way up to my shoulders.

He feints a kick, and I'm ready for the punch afterward.

Ready, but it doesn't do much of anything. Even a blocked hit rattles my teeth. He's just that big.

If you're going down anyway, you might as well go down swinging.

So I do.

I catch him across the jaw. Another time under his ribs. My hands go numb first, which means there'll be hell to pay in the morning.

If I survive to the morning.

He aims at the side of my head, and I get an arm up just in time to take the edge off. Fuck. *Fuck.* His other hand comes around next. My vision swims.

I duck to the back corner and keep moving to delay the next hits. Not forever. Mountain Man's steps feel like earthquakes as he approaches.

Block. Swing. Block *again.*

Head's starting to hurt. If he gets another direct hit

to the face, I'll be done. But that's why I came here, honestly. To be knocked unconscious.

If Mountain Man wants to do that, he'll have to work for it. He'll have to *invest*.

He's sweating now, not used to chasing people around the ring for this long. He backs off, both hands up, catching his breath.

I smile at him from behind the tape covering my bruises. Give him a come-hither wave.

He charges.

I wait him out until the last second, then stick out my foot and trip him.

Mountain Man goes down hard, and I fold my arms over my chest and roll my eyes. I pretend to check my watch while he pushes himself up off the floor. The crowd's laughter sounds like it's being filtered through broken glass.

See? I'm the favorite. They're all cheering for me.

Mountain Man's not.

I get my hands up, but he grabs lower on my torso. I'm up in the air, the faces around the ring a blur of color, and then the mat and the hard floor beneath rush up and smash into me.

I taste blood.

There's a whistle from far away. There aren't many rules in the ring, but one of them is that you can't bodyslam people.

If you let me stay...

The ref's face bulges into view. All the proportions are fucked. "Are you out?"

"Fuck no."

I hop to my feet, which earns me a deafening cheer.

"One strike," the ref calls, pointing at Mountain Man. He's got two left before I win by default.

But I'm not going to win by default.

Fuck this guy.

My torso is a mess of bruises and I can barely feel my hands. Why not go after him with everything I have?

I'm faster. That's the advantage. I concentrate on all the softest parts of him. There aren't many.

He punches back like I've genuinely pissed him off, which I have. I was supposed to crawl to the side of the ring and surrender after he broke all my bones on the mat.

As if this is the first time anyone's ever held a grudge.

As if I'm afraid of what comes next.

What's he going to do, lock me in his closet?

I laugh out loud, and oh, boy, he hates that. His knuckles crack into one of my temples and my vision dims. I'll be lucky to get out of this without a broken eye socket.

I'll be lucky to get out of this at all.

Pretend, Bristol says.

I'm not pretending now. This is who I am. This

monster in a boxing ring. This monster who's going to get himself killed by a human mountain just because it feels better than his sham of a life.

If I died, someone would have to tell her.

Who? The receptionist at Summit? Some anonymous person at the temp agency?

Fuck that *twice*. It's not just that there's nobody else to bail her out when her apartment caves in. It's that nobody's going to tell her that I let this bastard take me from her.

I'm not the one who leaves.

I'm the one who *stays,* goddamn it.

I don't want to go.

I don't know whether it's Bristol's voice or mine or somebody else's in my head. The words go off like a bomb. They separate out all the seconds of this fight like splinters of wood. Like freeze-frame photos of being hauled out of a dark closet and into the light.

I'm not letting him do this again.

I register shock on Mountain Man's face through a haze of red, and then I'm on top of him. Hit after hit. I sacrifice my knuckles to the cause. Every future mouse click.

He's not used to a left-handed fighter. That's obvious now. He keeps preparing for hits from the opposite side. Keeps failing to be ready.

I'm dimly aware that Mountain Man's fallen. That

he has one arm up to try to protect his face. That the crowd noise has become a sustained, bloodthirsty howl.

I hear the bell, but I don't stop.

He's down and tapping out, but I don't stop.

Blood drips down onto my hand, but I don't stop.

I can't.

Somebody pulls at my wrist. The ref, probably. *Fine,* I say. *I'm good.* But I keep throwing punches. We're not even yet.

Arms wrap around my shoulders and haul me away from the man I've beaten. Is this what it feels like when Sinclair tackles Emerson? Does it hurt this much?

Whoever it is drags me toward the ropes and turns me around. I blink away blood and try to focus. I'll be damned. I've never seen eyes like that before. Every shade of blue I can imagine. Like the entire ocean in one spot. It's the dark-haired guy from earlier. The one with the wife who will murder him for some kid Jason.

He's talking, but I can't hear him at first. The ocean stares into my eyes, searching for something.

Oh. He's scolding the ref.

"—see that one of your crew is about to snap? Should've called it earlier. Jesus Christ. Where's the closest hospital?"

The ref comes to my side, grabs my wrist, and thrusts my hand into the air. A roaring cheer echoes off the warehouse roof.

"You're banned," he shouts into my ear. "What the hell were you thinking?"

"Fine." More blood in my mouth. I spit it onto the mat. Someone presses money into my hands. My winnings. It's victory, but it doesn't feel like it. Bristol's not here. "How long?"

"How long are you *banned*?" The ref's incredulous. "For a month."

"Two weeks," I counter.

"Don't come back for a month," the ref warns. "I mean it, Will."

I get an argument together, but the dark-haired guy shouts for somebody named Nicholas. The one with the scar climbs up to the ropes.

"Help me get him down." An order to Nicholas from the dark-haired guy.

"I don't need help," I say.

Nicholas ignores this completely. The two of them help me over the ropes like it's the railing of a ship. Then I'm in a sea of people, being steered toward the exit. There are more guys with us by the time I step out into cool, fresh air. Both my ears ring. One of my ribs feels broken. Bruised, at least.

I head in the direction of my car. I *think* it's the direction of my car. If it isn't, I'll just keep walking until I find a place to sit down.

A minute later, headlights stretch out my shadow on

the concrete. A black SUV pulls up alongside me, and the dark-haired prick from inside jumps out. "Not a chance, hellion."

"Go away."

"Then I'd have to tell Ashley I left you for dead, and I'm not going to do that." He opens the passenger door and half-lifts, half-shoves me inside. "You have everybody?"

I don't have anyone, but he's not talking to me. He's talking to Nicholas, who has jogged up behind us. "They're all out."

"Send them to the ship. Tell Ashley I'll be back soon. Don't say a fucking thing to my brothers."

"Oh, like she's not going to tell them herself."

"Fuck you, Nicky." It sounds affectionate when the ocean guy says it like that.

"Fuck you, too."

Fuck me. Fuck all of us. I mean to get back out of the SUV, but I need a minute to catch my breath. The guy who's stronger than Sinclair—taller, too, what the hell—shuts my door and climbs into the driver's seat.

"No hospital."

He rolls his eyes. "Where, then?"

I give him Bristol's address.

Chapter Twenty-One
Bristol

A GOOD TIME to sort out one's feelings about her angry, kind, cold, unbelievably hot temporary boss is while washing dishes. Actually, it's a good time to work through just about anything. You can go through the motions of transforming dirty dishes into sparkling clean ones while your mind works.

I don't have to wash dishes anymore. Not as long as we live in this apartment. Not as long as the brand-new, top-of-the-line dishwasher from Will holds out.

I run the plates and cups and silverware under hot water anyway, turning them over and over until there's not a speck of lasagna left. Late-night rinsing. The twins have been asleep for a couple hours already.

Will's been all over the place. I've only known him for a little while. I *know* something's up, though. In my bones. In my soul. Whatever.

Those things he said today were something else.

How long would it have taken you to run the con to the end, Bristol? A month? A year? What would you let me do to you before you walked away?

He talks about time more than anyone I've ever met. About staying. About being locked in.

And the suggestion that I was angling for *more* time, a longer con that would ultimately end in me walking away with a bag full of money?

All I can think is that the scenario puts him in control of the timeline. He's the one who's cutting it off at two weeks. He's the one who's deciding.

Never mind that he's always been in control.

Or maybe it only seems that way.

My cell rings on the countertop. Unknown number. I wipe my hands on a dish towel that feels frankly luxurious and pick it up before it can stop ringing.

"Hi, this is Bristol."

There's a crackling, static sound, and then a voice: "Hey, little sister."

"Hey yourself." I smile at the pristine, empty sink. "I take it you have cell service for the next thirty seconds?"

My older brother, Sean, laughs. "A whole damn minute, if I can help it."

He's black ops, so when I told Will he wasn't around, I meant it. I have no idea what part of the world he's in half the time, and I always answer unknown numbers. He calls whenever he can.

"Are you doing okay?"

"The weather's nice. Scenery's picturesque." That's all he'll ever say, even when I can hear a thunderstorm in the background. "What the hell's going on over there? I got a message from Dad."

"Seriously?"

"An *email*." Sean scoffs. "Haven't had a chance to check for weeks. Something about the roof. Aren't you in the terrace of some duplex?"

"That was the last place. We're in an apartment in New York City now."

"Who's *we*?"

I sigh, stepping back from the sink and moving through the kitchen. Checking cupboards. Checking the fridge. We have all-new silverware and dishware. A fully stocked pantry. A fridge and freezer nearly at capacity with food that's been out of our budget for years.

"Me and Mia and Ben."

"Did that bastard have somewhere better to be?"

"I don't know. He took off the night the roof caved in. I haven't heard from him."

"Bristol." More static. "You can't keep doing this. Mom's dead. Dad's useless."

"Which means I have to take care of them. You know that."

"What I know is that you're not their mother. You've given up most of your life for Mia and Ben, and if this keeps up, you'll give up the rest, too."

"Aren't you the one who signed up to give your life for your country?" I let the cupboard *snick* shut.

"Damn it, Bristol."

"That's what I thought." Point to me. Sean can shut up about giving lives away.

"Do you need extra money to fix the roof?" There's a rustling sound over the line. "I can send the difference. Or the whole amount. Whatever you need."

Everywhere Will touched flushes hot. Embarrassment, definitely. Shame, maybe. And wanting more of him. I cough to cover it up. "Actually, I got an advance from work."

"An advance?" Somehow, from the other side of the world, my brother isn't buying this.

"Yeah."

"So it's working out, then?" A beat of silence. "The temp agency?"

"Oh, yes. Yeah. It's good."

Good, but my boss is on my mind twenty-four hours a day. Good, but he needed something from me today, and I'm not sure I gave it to him. Good, but it's also extremely fucked up.

"What's wrong?" Sean asks. He always hears it when I hesitate or try to bullshit him. We've talked on the phone almost more than we've spoken in person.

"Nothing for you to worry about."

"Bristol..."

"I'm just tired. Everything's fine. I'm figuring it out."

"What kind of temp agency gives out advances?"

"It wasn't the temp agency. It was my boss at the firm I'm working at."

The silence is definitely judgmental now. No boss in the world would give out an advance like this with no strings attached, and Sean knows it.

"Listen." A distant voice, far in the background. "You have to remember your goals. You always wanted to get out of there and go to the beach. Being some man's toy—"

"*Sean.*"

"—is not going to get you there."

"I know. I do." These calls never last long. They can't. I don't want to fight with him. "That's still the plan. Dad being gone so long is just a temporary setback. It's all going to work out."

There's a strange knock at the door. Almost muffled somehow. Like the person really has to try.

"You sure, Bristol?"

It comes again, sharper this time.

"Sean, I have to—"

"Time's up," he says. There are shouts in the background. "Gotta go. Love you."

The line goes dead, and I slide the phone back onto the countertop. It could be my dad at the door. It could also be people who want to do him harm. It could be anyone.

I rise on tiptoe to look through the peephole.

Then I'm scrambling for the deadbolt, fast as I can. My heart jumps up and down, demanding answers. Why is he here? And who the hell hurt him? Even with the warped view of curved glass, I could tell something was wrong. I open the door to reveal fresh bruises and blood.

"Oh my God, Will. What happened?"

He takes one look at me, grips the doorframe, and propels himself into the apartment. His hands are on me the next second, followed closely by his mouth on mine.

It would be a sweet kiss if I couldn't taste blood.

"I went to a fight," he says.

Will kisses harder, backing me into the wall, and I almost, *almost* fall into it and forget myself. Forget everything. Forget that he doesn't belong here.

This is what makes sense. This heat. This fury. The metallic taste of this fight he...

This fight he *went* to?

Will breaks away to suck in a breath, and I catch him wobbling. Unsteady on his feet.

I snap out of it. Back into the reality that he's bloodied and bruised and looks like hell. The twins can't wander out and find him like this. "You're hurt. You need to sit down."

"I really don't. Kiss me again."

A better person would probably refuse, but I can't do it. I put my hands on the sides of his face, noticing his pained blink, and lean in. I give him a soft brush of my lips, not wanting to hurt him.

Will's hands go to my waist. He shifts his weight toward me. It's even less clear now whether he's doing it to trap me against the wall or because he's going to fall on his ass.

"This way. Now."

It's not far to my bedroom. Will sits on the edge of the bed and looks up at me. "Did you bring me here so I'd fuck you on your own bed?"

"We are *not* fucking right now. You're still bleeding."

"But you have the nicest tits, Bristol."

"Don't be an ass. Just… stay there. Don't move."

Will flicks his eyes toward the ceiling. He hasn't moved when I get back from the bathroom with a warm washcloth and the first aid kit.

He watches me through slitted eyes. The eyes of a predator still fresh from the fight, adrenaline coursing through his veins. He'd be rough with me right now. I can feel his violence pulsing in the air around us. "You're beautiful and sweet and delicate. I'm going to break you."

"No, you're not."

"I am, Bristol. You should get away from me."

My heartbeat falters. I don't want to get away from

him. This debt I owe could cost me a lot more than my body. A *lot* more. "There's blood on your face. I need to clean it off so I can figure out where the cut is."

"There's probably multiple cuts."

And multiple bruises. "Then I'll find those, too. Tell me what happened."

"Already did." I bring the cloth to Will's forehead, and he hisses at the first contact. One of the cuts is up near his hairline.

"You said you went to a fight. What does that even mean?"

"What it sounds like."

"You look like you lost."

A sad, bitter smile. "I didn't lose."

My stomach sinks. I swipe antibiotic gel on the cut, then follow it with a bandage. On a hunch, I reach for the hem of his shirt and tug it up a few inches.

The breath goes out of me. More bruises than I've ever seen. Most of them too dark already to mean anything good.

"Will."

"Is this the part where we can finally fuck? You know that's why I came."

His eyes are on mine, and the blue is bright against the streak of blood on his cheek. Bright and *sad*. So sad it squeezes at my heart. I reach for him without thinking. Without planning.

I put my arm around his neck and pull him into a hug.

Will's body starts to lean into it. Starts to give in. But then he puts a hand on my shoulder and pushes me back. "Don't do that."

"Because it hurts?"

"Because that's not *for* me." Will's eyes go slightly unfocused, but they snap back again. It doesn't last.

"Hugs aren't for you?"

"Fuck no." A bitter laugh. "I've never liked them. Fistfights are what I like. Don't *hug* me, Bristol." His eyes drift toward the door, and he winces. "I'm going to lie down for a minute."

It's more of a fall toward the pillow, and not a very graceful one.

A worried pressure wraps around my lungs, but I ignore it. No time to be freaked out at times like these. I stick my hands into one of Will's pockets, then the next.

"I knew it." He closes his eyes, then opens them again. "I knew you'd try to take my pants off. You're not a good corporate whore, sweetheart. You're not supposed to let anybody come home with you."

I find his phone in the third pocket. There's a crack in the screen, but it's working.

"Code." I dangle it in front of Will's face. He gives it a wary look, like he's never seen it before. "Four numbers."

He picks up his left hand. It's all taped up. What the hell kind of fight was this? I'd bet the fifty thousand dollars I owe him that there are purple bruises underneath that tape. Four taps at the screen, and his hand falls back down to the bed. Will curses under his breath.

"What do you need with my phone?" He's already closed his eyes against the glow from the bedside lamp. It's not enough. Will slings an arm over his face. Curses again.

If he wasn't already pissed at me, he will be now.

I wish, with everything I have, that letting him stay was an option. It's not. Mia and Ben are asleep. I don't want them to run into him without a warning. And if this turns into an emergency, I can't leave them to take him to the hospital.

I think this might already be an emergency.

I open his Contacts app. The Favorites list pops up first. There are only two people on it. *Sinclair Leblanc. Emerson Leblanc.*

I put a hand over the ache in my heart and tap Sinclair's name.

Half a ring, and the call connects. "Tell me you got the right superyacht and you're in a better mood, asshole."

"Hi, is this Sinclair?"

Metal *clinks* in the background, like keys coming off a hook. "Yeah. Who has my brother's phone?"

"This is Bristol Anderson. I'm Will's..." *Corporate whore.* "...secretary."

And I'm calling because I saw you in a picture and you're the oldest. That has to mean something.

"Does he always make you work this late?" A door closes somewhere in the distance.

"No, actually. He came to my apartment a few minutes ago. Unexpectedly."

The sound on the other end of the line changes, like Sinclair has gone outside. "Is he too drunk to drive?"

"He's too beat up to drive. He said something about a fight."

"Okay." A car door closes. The engine turns over a second later. "Text me the address. I'll be right there."

CHAPTER TWENTY-TWO
Will

WELL, FUCK.

Everything feels terrible. My face. My gut. The shoulder that's pressing into the bed is on fire.

"Does that sound mean you're awake or dead?"

I force my eyes open. More pain. Sinclair looks down at me from the side of the bed, a glass in his hand.

It would probably be better if I was dead.

Takes me a few seconds to work up to words. "Hurts to move my jaw."

"It's not broken," he says briskly.

Feels broken. "What bed is this?"

"Guest bedroom in my rental."

"Thought you were staying in a hotel."

"Got sick of housekeeping coming in and out all the time, so I got something longer-term. Can you get up?"

Yes, but not without cursing myself and every person who's been involved in my continued existence.

Especially the guy who taught me to box. Fuck you, Eddie. If I'd been less good at it, Mountain Man would have taken me out early. I wouldn't be this fucked up. I wouldn't be banned.

I put my hands to my face and discover that it's better if I don't touch it at all.

"Here." Sinclair holds the glass out. "Drink this. It'll help."

I stare down into green mush. "No, it won't."

"It's a kale smoothie."

My stomach lurches. "Then it definitely won't help."

"Trust me."

It pisses me off enough that I grab the glass out of his hand and swallow an inch or two of the smoothie.

Swallow? Jesus. It's more like biting through it. Turns into choking it down. And then it turns into kale-flavored acid in the back of my throat.

"Fuck off with that." I shove the glass into Sin's hand. "Jesus Christ. You *drink* those?"

He peers at me like I'm not kale-heaving on the bed. "You look like absolute hell."

"Thanks."

"You want to tell me why you almost got yourself killed at an illicit fight club last night?"

I stand up in an effort to get my stomach to settle down, which doesn't help. I'm wrecked from head to toe. "Is that what Bristol told you?"

Not sure how she'd know, but anything's possible.

Sin points into the next room. I hobble in that direction and find a huge, overstuffed sofa with an ottoman. It's marginally better with my feet up.

My brother takes the cursed smoothie into the kitchen and puts it in the sink. Then he comes back and sits in a chair across from me, his feet next to mine on the ottoman.

"No. *You* told me about it after I collected your concussed ass from her apartment."

I frown at my feet on the ottoman. I remember Sin driving an SUV and a bunch of bright lights, but no conversation. "Who told you I had a concussion?"

"On-call doctor from a cute little medical boutique. She came with a leather doctor bag and everything."

"What the fuck, Sin."

"It was that or the ER. And you were a picky bastard who didn't want to be seen at a hospital. The doctor was good, anyway. She gave me a list of instructions. By the way, you can't go back to that damned warehouse for at least a month."

I laugh, which hurts, too. "I'm banned for a month."

Sin arches an eyebrow. "Because you got your ass kicked?"

My fist, cracking against the bones in Mountain Man's face. Again and again and again. I flex the bruised knuckles in my left hand and think of arms dragging me away and *not a chance, hellion* and Bristol's voice.

"I wasn't supposed to win the match. But after I got the guy on the ground, I couldn't stop."

Sin nods sagely. "Turned into Dad, didn't he?"

"I don't know."

Yes. For fragments of time, they were the same person. And I was the same person I've always been. A dangerous, violent monster who doesn't know when to stop.

"So." Sin folds his hands over his stomach. Part of me wishes he'd stop looking at me this way, all concerned, brotherly bullshit. But the other part thinks *finally, someone saw.* Saw what, exactly, I don't know. "Who's Bristol? She said she was your secretary."

"She's not. She's just a temp."

"You're full of shit." Sin cracks the smile that made him famous on Instagram. "You're telling me you dragged yourself half-dead to your *temp's* apartment in the middle of the goddamn night?"

"No. I got a ride. And then I dragged myself up three flights of stairs."

"What cab driver picked you up looking like that?"

"Wasn't a cab. Some guy from the warehouse. I didn't get his name."

Didn't need it. There was something familiar about him. He had guys willing to follow him out to sea, unless I hallucinated the parts about the ship and crew. Either way, he took care of his people. Even me, and I was nobody.

"But you got in a car with him?"

"Yeah, Sin, and I'm here to tell the tale. Stop pretending to care. You're not my mother."

He blinks, his eyes sliding away from mine. I *am* an asshole. Sin is objectively better than Mom. She never came back. She died instead, without another word to any of us.

"It's dangerous to get into cars with strangers," Sin intones. "Now tell me about Bristol."

I groan, shutting my eyes. "She's a temp at Summit for another four days. That's it."

"How long have you been in love with her?"

"I'm not in love with her," I snap. "I don't care about her at all."

"Ooookay." I open my eyes again to find Sin with his hands folded behind his head, a smug grin on his Instagram-star face. "Emerson fell in love first. Now you."

"Absolutely fucking not."

"Then why'd you go to her place?" Sin's eyes twinkle. "Why did you put up such a fuss about leaving?"

"I don't know, prick. Probably the concussion."

"Or true love."

I roll my eyes, which makes my head throb. "If you think this is love, then you should be scared shitless."

"Why?"

"Because you're the last brother left. That means you're next."

Sin scoffs, gently. "Love is for people like you and Emerson. Not for me. Ever."

I stare at him, eyes wide. "Do you even hear yourself? *Me and Emerson?* Because we have so much in common."

My brother shrugs. "You're both gluttons for punishment."

"Weird. I've never seen him at the warehouse."

"Come on, Will. The concussion didn't do *that* much damage."

"We're nothing alike."

Sin spreads his hands out in front of him like his palms are a scale. "You sign up for suicide matches at the warehouse. Emerson forces himself to walk fifteen blocks every time he comes into the city, and he insists on surfing every day."

"Yes, and you jump off cliffs. You visit active war zones. Wow, you're right, Sin. You're *so* different. No one could ever love you."

He waves me off. "Don't let it keep you up at night. In fact, if you go through with your merger, you'll be too busy for both of us."

The accusation stings, though I have no idea why. It's not like we stuck together after I graduated college. It's not like Sin didn't go to LA. It's not like Emerson didn't shut himself into his house to an extent that I didn't realize until Daphne came into the picture.

He unfolds his hands from behind his head and taps at one knee. "Don't do it."

"Don't do what?"

"Don't go through with the merger."

I shake my head. Mistake. "Excuse me?"

Sin leans forward and clasps his hands like he's listening hard at one of his investigative journalist interviews. "You're fucked in the head from having so much money. It's getting to you."

"*Money* is getting to me?" I shove my hand into one of my pockets. The denim feels like sandpaper on my ruined knuckles. There's a stray hundred at the bottom of my pocket, and I dig it out and hold it up. "This is the only thing that separates me from being a complete fucking monster, Sin. *Money.* See? It's a thin goddamn line."

He reaches over the ottoman, plucks it out of my hand, and tears it in half.

"What the *fuck.*"

Sin drops the halves of the hundred-dollar bill, letting them flutter to the rug. "You have more money than you need. A hundred dollars doesn't make a difference to you. A *thousand* doesn't make a difference. Don't do the merger."

"You don't understand. I need more money, not less.

I don't want to be a monster."

I already *am* a monster. That's what he doesn't get. But the more money that stands between me and everybody else, the safer they are.

He smiles, eyes soft, like I'm being ridiculous and sad. "You're not, Will."

"You're only saying that because you don't know that I'm blackmailing my temp for sex."

Sin's eyebrows go up. "Bristol?"

"Yeah. I fucked her in the conference room yesterday."

Even the way Emerson went after Daphne was less monstrous than this.

"Okay." Sin nods. He doesn't look nearly as horrified as I want him to. He doesn't look nearly as awed at how depraved I am. "Maybe you are a bit unconventional. But if you really like her, why not take her on a date?"

"She'd get the wrong idea."

"What wrong idea?"

"That I'm like that. Capable of a normal life. Kisses and hugs and wedding bells and all that shit."

Sin looks at me for a long time. "You want a hug, Will?"

"No. I want to go back to the warehouse. That's where I belong. In a fistfight, not going on dinner dates with innocent women."

"Pretty sure you're banned."

"My car's over there somewhere. I have to go home and change. I have meetings all day."

"No, you don't."

"Yes, I fucking do."

"I called and said you'd be out." Sin stands up and stretches, then wanders toward the kitchen. "Go shower. I'll find clean clothes. You're staying here for the next twenty-four hours."

"The fuck I am."

"Doctor's orders. Even if you can stand up long enough to shower, you're in no shape to drive."

"I'm fine."

He pokes his head out of the kitchen and taps his temple. "That guy rang your bell. You have a concussion. You're not even supposed to sleep for longer than three hours without somebody waking you up to be sure you're still alive."

"Who the hell has time for that?"

"Same person who had time last night." Sin gives me a pointed look, the bastard. "I'm a little offended, Will. I was up with you every three hours, and all you wanted to talk about was Bristol."

Chapter Twenty-Three
Bristol

THERE'S A SCALE, you know?

There's *bad* like wondering if your boss is going to fire you because he found out you stole fifty thousand dollars from his company. And *bad* like wondering if your boss is going to fire you because he wants to prove that you mean nothing to him.

There's *bad* like wondering if your boss is going to make you get on your knees in the conference room in front of a bunch of strange men, and *bad* like wondering if your boss is going to die from wounds he sustained in a mystery fight.

There's *bad* like only having five days left to pay him back, and *bad* like his office sitting empty for two of them while you wait and worry.

The waiting should be over tomorrow morning, at least. Will sent a company-wide email this afternoon saying he'd be back in the office tomorrow morning.

It's not soon enough.

I felt awful for sending him away with his brother after he showed up at my apartment. Guilt gnawed at me the rest of the night. I couldn't sleep. I kept checking my phone, hoping for updates, but there weren't any.

Who would think to text me? Not Sinclair, Will's dark-haired brother. He at least agreed that someone with a medical license should check to see if Will had taken surgery-level damage. They went out the door to apartment 306 while Will insisted he'd never felt better.

"Oh, really?" Sinclair pulled Will out into the hall just before the door closed. "That why your pupils are different sizes and you can't keep track of the conversation?"

"What conversation?" Will said.

The bus bumps to a stop, brakes squealing. I climb off and head around the bus shelter.

I don't know if I believe that Will is going to be in his office. He was *hurt*. People don't bounce back from that level of bruising and blood in two days.

I frown at the courtyard, with its bumpy, ruined concrete and the ancient, net-less basketball hoop, but I'm seeing Will at the door. He didn't seem surprised to be hurt the way he was. He seemed resigned to it. Almost relieved.

The bottom of my heart pinches. I wish I could have taken him to the doctor myself. I wish I could have asked more questions.

I wish I understood.

Building C's door swings smoothly on the frame when I pull it open. Somebody that Will hired probably oiled the hinges. They replaced the kickplate, too.

Old habit makes me turn toward the stairs, but no. The elevator works now. Because of Will Leblanc. I push the call button and the doors open to let me on.

That's the screwed-up part, right? That I want to understand how he won a fight and still looked completely battered. I want to know what makes Will, the wealthiest person I've ever met, react to a hug like a hornet sting.

I want to see him.

I've wanted to see him since the door of 306 closed behind him. Wanted it so much that heat builds behind my eyes every time I think about him.

My life is always about decisions like that. The lesser of two evils. The more sensible of situations that aren't sensible at all. I'm used to giving things a chance. I'm used to forging ahead even when I wish I could make any other choice.

It's a quick elevator ride. A matter of seconds.

I take a breath before the doors open and gather myself. The twins will be home from school already. They'll need help with homework. Something to eat for dinner. Clean clothes to wear to bed.

Not a worried, quiet older sister.

I lift my chin as the elevator doors open, put on a fake-it-'til-you-make-it smile, and step into the hall.

A hand clamps down over the smile, pinching my lip to my teeth in a sharp burst of pain. I make a shocked noise into his palm. What the hell? In the hallway? Here?

My uncoordinated struggle against his grip doesn't make much of a difference. He drags me backward, fifteen feet in the opposite direction of apartment 306. One of my heels catches on the industrial hallway carpet and wrenches my ankle on its way off my foot.

He stops at an alcove. Yanks me into it.

I shout into his palm. I just need one person to open their apartment door. One person to see that this isn't right. Anybody.

A blow lands on the side of my head. The impact throbs into my brain and for a second I can't breathe.

It's terrible, because all my muscles burn cold with adrenaline. I want to run more than I've ever wanted anything in my life, but the analytical part of my mind—the one that budgeted for gas-station food on the road and figured out how many nights we could last at the cheapest motel in town—knows there are no options.

I'll never get the door to 306 unlocked before he catches up with me.

At best, I'll get my phone out of my purse. He's not going to let me type in my passcode and make a call.

The police aren't going to come here in a hurry.

My number one priority is to stay alive no matter what happens in this alcove. Mia and Ben can't find my dead body out here. They just can't.

I've been pushing against his arm, against his hand, but I stop. As much as I can.

Another hit to the side of my head. My cheek, really.

"Don't scream," he says.

I don't know whether to nod or shake my head, so I just stand perfectly still.

He waits a few seconds, then lifts his hand away from my mouth.

"You owe me fifty thousand dollars."

My skin pulls tight. The man with the gun. The man who threatened the twins. "My dad said he paid you back. I gave him the money to pay you back."

"Next time you run errands for your daddy, you might want to deliver the cash yourself. He didn't give me a goddamn dime. He still owes me."

"Then I'm not the person you want. He'll be back soon. When he is, you can talk to him about it."

"I've waited long enough for that prick to come around. You're going to find the money." He moves his arm, and I flinch, expecting another hit. But his hand goes around my wrist and then my arm is jammed behind my back. It hurts. Shoulder to wrist. Every muscle and bone and ligament. "You're going to find it *fast.*"

"I can't."

"You don't have a choice." He gives my wrist a shake. "I've been watching this place. All kinds of people in and out, fixing things. You know somebody with money."

"My dad—"

"Left you here."

"He's coming back."

"When?"

"Tomorrow night. He got a job. His shift ends at nine." I throw my panicked heart into it. *My dad has a job. He's coming back after work tomorrow. I'm telling the truth. Believe me.*

"Then that's when I'm coming to talk to him. Either he'll hand me the money, or you will. If you don't—"

"You'll kill him?"

"Those kids in there are cute," he mentions. "Are they your brother and sister?"

All the air evaporates from my lungs. They feel like flat balloons. "They're kids. Leave them out of this."

"How long do you think the boy would survive without that little redhead? Or do you think he'd lose his mind as soon as she was dead?"

"*Don't.*"

"Think of it as motivation." He shifts his weight, and I tense up again. "One of them could be worth fifty thousand dollars."

"If you *touch* them—"

He cuts me off with a sharper hit to my head. Same spot as before. Then he turns me, and a fist goes into my gut. I fold to my knees and get my hand to the alcove wall.

The man is nothing but a shadow above me.

Look, every hopeful shred of me says. *Look at his face so you can give a description.*

But who would I give it to? I'm a criminal as much as he is.

Fingers dig into my hair, forcing my face into the corner of the alcove. Too late. Can't look now.

"Nine o'clock tomorrow night. Have your daddy waiting with the money, or you and those kids can pay the debt."

He pulls tighter, my scalp screaming, and lets go.

Quick steps move down the hall. There's a metallic screech as he hits the push bar on the stairwell door.

My phone vibrates in my purse. If it's Will, I can't answer. He might come over here, and he's already been beaten to a pulp this week.

Or he might *not* come, and then I'll be a broken-hearted fool who has twenty-nine hours to find another fifty thousand dollars.

I pull out my phone.

The screen reads **Mia & Ben Anderson.**

I got them a prepaid phone a couple years ago in case of emergencies.

Just... please. No more emergencies right now. I need another moment to collect myself.

I give it one more ring. "Hello?"

"Are you almost home?" Mia's worried and pretending not to be. "We're okay, but I thought you were going to be here by now."

There's going to be a bruise on my face. I have to head it off before it scares them. I won't let this touch them.

"You know what? I took a little tumble at the bus stop. I hit my head." I give a laugh that sounds shaky and not very convincing. I hope my sister believes it.

"You *did?*"

"I'll probably have a bruise, but I'm fine." I get my feet under me. My gut aches when I stand up. My right shoe is sprawled on the hallway carpet. I flip it upright with my toes and step in. That ankle feels weak. Sore. I put on a smile. "You guys are probably starving. What can I make for dinner?"

Chapter Twenty-Four
Will

NOBODY AT THE office wants to look at me.

It's probably a sign that Sinclair was right. I should have called out the rest of the week.

But fuck him. He knows as well as I do that the bruises will look worse before they look better.

I'm not missing Bristol's last two days because I got my ass kicked. My vision is almost back to normal. I don't want to throw up in the shower.

Getting to the office at seven felt more like torture than a normal workday, but I don't care.

There's plenty to catch up on. Contracts that need my approval. Deals to vet. A string of emails from Greg about the merger.

Our lawyers were busy while Sinclair woke me up all goddamn day and night. They've translated all my demands into legalese. There's a section just for the superyacht.

And a note in an email from Greg.

Included all your requirements for company culture, hiring, etc. Added a clause that gives you the option to transfer management and infrastructure to us at any point.

It has a knowing tone to it that frankly I fucking hate. It's a wink to the idea that I'm going to want to climb aboard my new superyacht the second the ink is dry on the documents and sail off to the Bahamas. Or *Paris.*

That's the last thing I want to do. I want it even less than I want to take orders from Finn Hughes.

People move back and forth outside my office door. Christa's the first one to risk it.

She pauses on the other side of the desk, looking at me the same way she'd look at a balance sheet covered in red ink. "Jesus, Leblanc."

"The Prince of Peace had nothing to do with it."

"Tell me the guy who did that to you got carted away in a cop car."

"He didn't, because I won. And stop staring."

She narrows her eyes. "Should you even be here? There's no way in hell you're supposed to be looking at a computer screen."

"It's fine. The business won't run itself."

It's not that fine, actually. The light from the screen feels like sand in my eyes and an ache in my skull. That could also be from the bruising.

"We could've handled things for the rest of the

week."

I turn my head back to the computer and catch her wincing out of the corner of my eye. "It's not going to be a problem."

Christa taps her fingernails against her mug. Red fingernail polish flashes in my peripheral vision and the ceramic *click click click* has an echo that makes my head hurt more. "Did you respond to Hughes yet?"

"I'm about to. Anything else you need me to look at first?"

My CFO hesitates. *Click click click.* "Nope. I'll be in my office."

"Good."

She leaves, and I stare at my email for another ten minutes. It hurts. The concussion's the least of it. Where the hell is Bristol?

Another five minutes go by. She's officially three minutes late.

I'm one minute from stalking down to the sidewalk and waiting for her at the front entrance when I hear her voice outside my door.

"Oh, no," she's telling somebody else. "Not a big deal. I'll check it out in just a minute."

Her voice gets softer, retreating. She's going to get my coffee. The email I was going to write seems impossible now. I'm not sure how I was going to start the damn thing.

It's more pressing to decide what I'm going to say to her when she walks in, smelling like sweet citrus and borrowed time.

I feel her at the door the instant before her movement registers. Bristol crosses the office with the same brisk pace she always uses and leans in over my desk.

"Morning, Mr. Leblanc." The coffee mug makes contact with the coaster.

And she turns it, putting the handle exactly where it should be for me to pick it up with my busted left hand.

I follow her fingertips from the mug to her wrist and up her arm. I have to apologize for more than being a jackass this time. I probably got blood on her sheets. I probably scared her.

It wasn't the way I wanted to scare her.

"Bristol, I—"

Her lovely green eyes are set off by the embarrassed flush on her cheeks. Bristol's lower lip is caught between her teeth. But what stops me dead and punches out my completely inadequate apology is the bruise on her face.

It skims her temple and goes down to her cheekbone.

I'm only aware of standing up because my perspective changes. I find myself looking down at the bruise, leaning all the way over the desk to reach for her. Take her chin in my hand. Turn her so more window light falls on the place where someone hit her.

My head pounds, but it's nothing to do with the

concussion and everything to do with rage spiking my blood pressure.

"Bristol." She closes her eyes, and I don't let go. "Who hurt you?"

I get a breath of citrus as she turns, pulling herself out of my hands. She goes to the door and closes it. I go around to the other side of the desk, but Bristol stops just out of my reach and draws herself up to her full height.

Two can play that game. I tower over her, arms crossed. In another minute my fists will be vibrating with fury.

"It's just a bruise." Her voice is soft and calm and reasonable. "Mind your own business."

My hands flex. I ball them back up. "This *is* my business."

"I'm a temp."

"A temp who owes me fifty thousand dollars. A temp who's mine for the next two days. You're my business, Bristol."

She lifts her chin, tears bright in her eyes. "You never told me how you got *your* bruise. You didn't tell me how you got the new bruises, either."

"That's totally different."

"No, it's not."

I can't do this. Can't keep my distance. I take one big step and force her to look up at me. I'm an inch from her skin and her heat and her cheap, pretty skirt suit. "Who the fuck did this to you? They'll be dead by sunset."

Her eyes go wide, and it reminds me of her brave terror during the performance review and the way she cried afterward. Maybe it's still me she's afraid of. Or maybe she's afraid for whoever's going to die as soon as I learn his name.

Bristol takes a wavering breath. "Please don't. Murder isn't good."

Murder is the only good response to the darkening bruise on soft, delicate skin. I'd love nothing more than to murder the bastard who did it and twenty of his closest friends. Right here, where Bristol can count their last breaths.

I won't even come close if she doesn't tell me what happened.

You never told me how you got your bruise.

That faint nothing of a bruise I had on her very first day. I couldn't find it now if I tried.

Fine. I'll make a deal with her. If I get the asshole's name out of this, it'll be worth telling her who I am.

My forearms ache. I want my hands up in front of my face. Admitting this to Bristol feels like going into the ring blindfolded. Like knowing that the human body has too many soft, vulnerable pieces to defend all at once.

"There are some warehouses down by the city docks that host fight nights."

A wrinkle appears in her brow. "Like wrestling?"

"Like boxing. Most of the events are… structured. I go on the nights that anyone can get into the ring. There aren't nearly as many rules."

Bristol's eyes flicker over the bruises on my face. Over the expensive shirt that hides even uglier marks. I know what she's seeing. I know it doesn't make any sense.

Her eyes meet mine again. "How did you get into that?"

"I joined a frat when I was in college. That was when I learned about the warehouses. We'd go as spectators, drinking and betting and generally being menaces to society."

That beer-soaked crowd of memories is like an arm banded across my chest. I'll never tell Bristol, never tell *anyone*, that I joined that goddamn fraternity because I was desperate for normalcy.

Even the pretend version.

Sure, I have my brothers. But I wanted friends who didn't know the first thing about being locked in a closet. Who'd never choked on fear at the sound of footsteps. Who never had to watch their next-oldest brother allow himself to be tortured into a lifetime of panic attacks if it meant keeping the youngest one safe.

They broke themselves for me, and I've never been able to forgive myself. Because all that suffering was for nothing. I learned how to be tough. I learned how to survive. And I became a monster despite their best efforts.

They know it.

I know it.

And deep down, they'll never forgive me for it, either.

I clear my throat. "After graduation, a bunch of the guys stayed in the city. Got into finance. We still went to the warehouse to bet on the matches. One night I put my name in and climbed into the ring."

Bristol inhales. "Did you win?"

"No. The other guy beat the hell out of me."

"Like this?"

Nothing like this. That night didn't make the top five worst beatings of my life. It felt familiar, actually.

Felt like home.

"I didn't go down easy, if that's what you're asking. After I climbed out of the ring, a guy named Eddie approached me. An underground trainer. He said I had talent." My laugh takes me by surprise. The sound throbs in my temples. I didn't have talent. I had experience. But I don't say that to Bristol, either. "Then he said that if I didn't want to get killed, I needed practice."

Bristol swallows. "Did you take him up on it?"

I give her the same cocky showman smile I use in the

ring. "Of course I did. I never stopped going back. And now I'm one of the best."

"But you're all beat up, Mr. Leblanc."

"Will." I know I'm crossing a line. I don't care.

Her breath catches. "You got *really* hurt, Will."

"That's the point."

Bristol's mouth drops open. She's absolutely gorgeous, even when she's horrified. "Why?"

"Because it feels right."

"To get hit? To get *punched*?"

It sounds so fucked up, when she says it like that. "I prefer my human contact to come through fighting. Fucking, if that's not available."

Bristol nods. "Is that why you freaked out when I hugged you? Because you're scared of hugs?"

I don't mean to snort at her like a total prick. It just happens. "When I *what*?"

She looks at me, all sad and solemn. "You had some strong opinions about it when you came to my apartment."

My memories of her apartment are dim. I certainly don't remember a hug, or a meltdown. I remember pain. That's it.

"Fine. Whatever. Tell me who hit you. Was it your fuckboy of a father? Because I'll hunt that bastard down."

"It wasn't him. He's an asshole, but he's not violent."

She sighs, and I see how tired she is. How this appearance at the office is all a show. "It was the man who's looking for him. He wanted to send a message through me."

"And what's his name?"

"I don't know. I didn't see his face. He caught me when I was getting off the elevator." Bristol swallows even harder, and I will not, I will *not*, take her in my arms. I won't. Because I'll sit down on the floor holding her and never get up again. "And anyway, Will, you can't do this. You can't just come into my life and control things and murder people and pretend it doesn't mean anything. You know that, right?"

"I'm not pretending. I'm not going to settle down and have babies with you."

Her eyes flash, and those tears get brighter. Bristol's heartache is a slap to the face. Shouldn't be much, but it hurts on bruised skin. "I didn't ask for that, but okay."

"I'm not doing that with anyone, but especially not you."

"Will."

"You deserve somebody better, sweetheart. I'm not that guy. I'm a monster. You don't want me. I promise."

"Why are you telling me this?"

"Because I'm coming to your place after work."

Bristol's hands lift, palms up, pure exasperation. "For what?"

"To figure out a plan. A different apartment. Security. Whatever's necessary."

"For now?"

Because tomorrow is her last day at Summit. I don't give a fuck about her temp contract, but it's a good excuse. It's a good excuse to never see her again, even if the thought makes me feel hollow.

"For now."

Chapter Twenty-Five
Bristol

At ten to five, I knock on the door to Will's office. He's on the phone with one of the guys from Hughes Financial Services, but I can't pay any attention to the words coming out of his mouth.

Fight nights. In a *warehouse*.

Will's sitting there, handsome and pressed and covered in awful bruises. He carries on the conversation like none of it hurts. I know it does. It has to. He's not made of stone.

Or maybe he is. I don't know. I don't know much of anything.

I know even less than I did before he told me about those boxing matches. That's not the entire story. He didn't discover at the age of twenty-two that he'd rather be punched than hugged. There's no way.

And I haven't had more time to negotiate. He only told me those things because he wanted a name.

Will picks up a pen and writes something on one of his white legal pads in halting strokes. His hand must be killing him. Then he holds up the message.

Go home, it reads. *I'll be right there.*

You know what? I'll ask him about all of this later. Somehow, I'll find the time.

We'll be having a different conversation at the apartment. The one where I tell him my dad's been gone since the storm and I'm beginning to think he's not coming back.

It's going to be fine.

We're going to figure something out, and then I'll take the advice I'm constantly giving to the twins and give it a chance.

Whatever *it* is.

I'm on high alert all the way home from Summit. I skip the elevator and climb the steps to the third floor, listening on every landing.

The hallway's empty.

I'm turning the key in the lock when Mia giggles. It's a real laugh. A happy one. The door opens on Mia and Ben in the living room. He's got one of her books in his hands, and from the grin on his face, he's been reading to her.

Mia always takes this as a hilarious joke, because books are her thing. Numbers are his. But Ben will go along with just about anything if it makes Mia happy.

"Bristol!" Mia jumps off the couch and comes over for a hug. Ben's right behind her. "We're hungry."

"I knew you would be. How was school?"

"I got to spend an extra twenty minutes in the library." Mia's proud. More library time is always a victory.

"And I didn't." Ben's joking. Cheerful.

Everything's looking up.

"Okay. Food." I head into the kitchen and hang up my purse on a brand-new hook by the cupboards. Mia and Ben trail after me like puppies. They're fully capable of demolishing a snack drawer without any outside help, but they've been careful with the restocked kitchen. I think they want it to stay nice. "What do you guys want?"

"Spaghetti." Both of them at once.

"Perfect." I reach into one of the lower cupboards for a pot and start filling it in the sink. Ben brings the salt grinder from the table and puts it next to the stovetop. "I'll do meatballs, too." The kind Will bought for us are fancy despite being frozen. "Oh, and I wanted to tell you. My boss—"

There's a knock at the door. Loud. Confident. Almost sharp.

Mia jumps at the sound, and Ben grabs her elbow and backs up.

"Guys, it's okay. It's just Will. I was about to tell you

that he's coming over to talk to me." Mia's gone so pale it breaks my heart. This is too much for a ten-year-old. Will's right. We need a new place, or we need real security. I can't leave it to him indefinitely, but first, I need him in the apartment with us so Mia and Ben can see that it's going to be fine. "We were going to go over a couple things."

I rise on tiptoe to look through the peephole. *Wrong,* a soft voice announces in my mind. But I'm committed to the act of opening the door. I'm *not* wrong. Will said he would be right here.

It's open less than two inches when my body catches up with my mind.

It's not Will.

Not Will at all.

It's a man in a dark jacket, tall and muscled and furious. He's huge, but too thin in the face. Glittering eyes. A flat, disgusted expression, like a snake. A gun.

I shove at the door to slam it, but he blocks it with his palm. "I'm here to talk to your father."

It's him. The man from the hallway. Probably the man who beat up Dad before. I step in front of the gap in the door. "I told you he wouldn't be back until later."

His smile is all teeth, and my stomach jitters through my feet and into the floor. "Thought you might be a con artist, too. Thought it might be better if I got here early and waited for him."

He puts his hand on the gun.

This part's over. If I try to close the door in his face, he'll shoot, and probably keep shooting until he's inside the apartment. I won't have him stepping over my dead body to terrorize the twins.

"Fine." I throw the door open with every scrap of confidence I've stolen from my dad over the years and gesture inside. "Come in and wait for him. I'd rather not leave the door just open to anyone."

The man rolls his eyes at my irritation. "Aren't you feisty? You weren't like this yesterday."

"You didn't use your manners and knock on the front door yesterday."

"That all it takes with you? Good manners?"

His grin slithers into a leer, and he pats the gun at his waist absently. Affectionately. My heart throws out all its cards and flops helplessly to the table, begging for the rest of my body to realize there's a threat. Here. Now. *Run.*

There's not going to be any running. Not yet. The twins have backed themselves into the far corner of the kitchen. I've never seen the whites of their eyes so huge.

"Hi, honey." The man's zeroed in on Mia's red hair. I could throw up on his shoes. Vomit all my anger and disgust onto the black, beat-up sneakers. "Is your dad going to be home soon?"

Mia's eyes land on mine. I can't nod at her. It would

be too obvious.

I go with a smile instead. A single corner of my mouth.

"Yes." My sister's chin goes up, and it kills me just as surely as a bullet would. That small, defiant *yes* will play on repeat in my head for the rest of my life. She shouldn't have to be this brave.

"How's his new job going?"

Mia hesitates.

"It's fine." Ben tightens his arm around her. "He's doing a good job."

The man who's here to ruin our lives smiles again, and my pulse is so fast it's fleeing the scene. Like packing up late at night while somebody pounds on the door. Like running to a rusted-out car with the twins' little hands in mine, one on either side, a backpack for all three of us banging against my back.

"Where does he work?"

Ben opens his mouth to answer.

A knock on the door rescues him.

It's Will. I know, because the noise is slightly off, like he's knocking with his right hand. He threw too many punches with his left.

I don't make a move. Don't want to do anything sudden. The asshole with the gun takes it out of his waistband, the barrel pointing toward the floor. He looks from me to the twins.

Another knock. More insistent.

"Answer it." He waves toward the door with the gun. "Tell whoever that is to go the hell away."

I head in his direction, going out of my way to crowd him. He backs up. I'm still between him and the twins when I reach the door and open it a few inches.

Will stands in the hall, eyes dark with worry and suspicion.

"Hi. I can't actually talk right now. Go away, and I'll call you later."

He tries to look behind me, into the apartment. "Did something come up?"

Yes. A man with a gun who's standing behind me right now. We could all end up dead, because my dad's not coming home and I don't have fifty thousand dollars in cash on me.

I look him in his gorgeous, blue-green eyes, praying he'll understand. Please, please understand. "No, everything's fine. My mom is home."

Bitter disappointment shadows his eyes, but it's chased away by a blank withdrawal in the space of a heartbeat. He might not remember the story about the postcard on my wall. The trip we never got to take. I don't think he remembers half the conversation we had after his fight, much less what I said while he fucked me in the conference room.

And then—

Understanding lights in his eyes like fire. He takes a

step back from the door and shrugs. "Okay. I'll call you later."

I push the door closed. Move slowly and carefully toward the twins. In the hallway, Will's footsteps retreat, getting softer and softer.

The push bar on the stairwell door squeaks.

It slams shut.

My eardrums feel tight with how hard I'm listening. How hard I'm believing that he'll come back. That he really did understand. That he'd never leave me here.

"Good work." The asshole shoves his gun back into his waistband. "Now, where were we? Oh. You were going to tell me which place in this city hired your thief of a father. Because I'm not sure—"

The apartment door bursts open, the noise so loud I'm sure it's come off the hinges, and Will races inside.

Mia screams. It's high, supercharged terror and I rush for the twins, throwing myself in front of them.

Will's at the gunman so fast he doesn't have time to reach for the gun. He looks like a nightmare with all his bruises and height and speed.

I've seen my dad try and fail to hold his own in a fistfight. I've never seen anything like Will Leblanc in a real life-or-death situation.

The other guy scrambles, his hands useless, for all of a second before Will hits him.

I've never been a fan of violence. Never liked wrestling on TV or fights outside shitty apartments or how my dad could never win.

But Will's left hook is both beautiful and devastating.

Mia screams again, when fist meets face and the gunman goes down hard. I can't tell if he's reaching for his gun or his head when Will scrapes him off the floor and hits him again. Blood from his nose streams down and darkens the collar of his shirt.

The gunman tries for one, weak hit. Will brushes it away and punches him in the gut, all the force of his body rotating into the movement.

This man seemed so strong in the hallway with his hand over my mouth, but now he folds like crumpled money. The fight is lost. His face is covered in blood, and his head lolls to the side. If it weren't for Will's hand on his shoulder, he'd be laid out.

It's over.

But Will's not done.

Chapter Twenty-Six
Will

THERE'S NO MONEY now.

There are no hundred-dollar bills to hold me back.

No ref, and no ring, and no rules.

Only me and this motherfucker and a haze over my vision like blood, like pain, like *I'll make you wish you were dead.*

I'll make him wish he was dead.

Every time I hit him, he shows me more of his weak spots. I pummel all of them. It's like an investment. Like a contract. Go over every line of the goddamn thing and take it apart.

I'm taking this guy apart.

My fist slips on blood. Does he think he's walking out of here again? Does he think he'll ever touch anybody again? Does he think he'll lock me in? Is that what he thinks?

Ring all the bells you want. Ban me from the warehouse forever. This isn't going to happen again. Not to Bristol.

Will, she says. Calls me back. *Stop.*

I pull him toward me by the front of his shirt. Drag him up to his feet. He's dangling. Barely there. One more hit. Ten more.

There's a hand on my arm.

I angle my fist toward it. My stance toward it. Everything toward that touch. Nobody's going to stop me. Not this time. The kitchen rotates around me, frame by frame by frame, refrigerator, sink, cupboard. I'll fight them too. I'll fight everybody. I'll end it.

Bristol's face comes into view.

Every hair on my body pulls up tight.

Bristol.

Bristol with her green eyes and her dark hair and her bruise. Bristol with her soft touch. Bristol in the path of my fist.

Her voice wasn't in my head. It was real.

Terrified sobs break through the red filter over my eyes and jolt my heart into a painful, guilty rhythm. Horror tastes like blood, like a throat scraped raw from screaming. I snap my teeth shut against bile.

How could I even for a second think about hitting her? How could I decide to fight without looking to see who was there? How could I ever let her get this close?

Weight tugs at my right hand.

The guy's slumped over. He's been out for a while. I'm the one who kept making him get up. Kept giving myself excuses to do more damage.

I drop him and he falls straight down. Doesn't make any noise on impact. *You should have lowered him,* that voice says, but I don't want to touch him anymore. I'll kill him, if I haven't already.

"Will," Bristol says.

I know better than to let her touch me. But that *sobbing.* Who's doing that? Not Bristol.

The kitchen rotates again as I turn my head and see them.

Children.

Bristol's sister with her bright red hair and her brother with a chalk-white face. They're cowering in the corner, his arms wrapped around her. But I can still see her eyes. She's afraid to turn her back on me.

Because I'm a monster.

A monster with a fucked-up face and bloodied hands. My dad's hands.

I'm not like him. I *am* him.

There's no money as a buffer now. No money as a façade. No money as a security blanket.

Those kids are afraid of *me.*

"Will." A gentle pull at my arm turns me away from them and back toward Bristol. Her eyes shine. "Are you okay?"

Am *I* okay? I just killed a man in front of her. Maimed him at minimum. There's nothing wrong with me. I feel fine.

Except that Bristol's jittery. So is the rest of the apartment behind her. Not an earthquake. My teeth, chattering. Fuck, that *hurts*. The bones of my skull are rattling too and there's a strange pressure in my head.

No. In my chest.

No. It's everywhere.

It's just adrenaline and old memories. It's nothing.

I could have hit her. I could have hurt her.

What was I thinking, coming here? Who did I think I was, letting her work as my temp?

Bristol puts one of her small, clean hands on mine. "I think you should sit down."

All my ribs are cracked open. My heart doesn't fit. It's a useless muscle now, and it bursts from the pressure. From her kindness. From the awful mistake she's making.

She's worried about me.

Me.

I was a goddamn fool. I thought there was nothing worse than a woman leaving. I've been so sure of it. For as long as I can remember.

But it was an unfounded fear.

The nightmare is a woman who stays.

The nightmare is Bristol, touching me like this, understanding in her eyes when she can never understand.

She's not going to walk away from me. She's never going to leave.

I have to leave her. I have to save her.

Because there's hope for Bristol Anderson. She's sweet and smart and determined and the world is going to love her.

There's no hope for me.

Her sister's sobs beat themselves into my head. Hope for all of them, if I leave them be.

I'm afraid to move. No other choice. I'm too close to Bristol. I could hurt her.

But I'm a weak motherfucker after all. I let her touch me for another heartbeat. Another two.

And then I ease my hand away from hers.

"Don't come any closer."

Bristol shakes her head, stepping in anyway. I back up. That puts me closer to the twins, and I can't be there either. If Mia screams again my head will split in two. I'm about to lose teeth as it stands. I have too much adrenaline and not enough air.

I don't trust myself. They shouldn't trust me, either.

I angle around Bristol, giving her a wide berth. "Stay over there. With them. Where I can't reach you."

"Will, please. You're—"

"I'm going to take care of this. There are things that

have to happen now." Cops, unfortunately. I take out my phone. This fucking thing is rattling, too. I squeeze it in one fist so I can see the screen to dial.

First call is to my private security firm. The one that staffs my apartment building and the Summit offices. My jaw aches from forcing my teeth to be still long enough to get the orders out.

"We'll have an advance team there in twenty minutes," the man on the other end of the line says.

I dial 9-1-1 next.

"Nine-one-one. What's your emergency?" A woman's voice. Warm. Collected.

Me. I'm the emergency. Send as many people as you have to get me the fuck out of here and keep me away from Bristol Anderson.

"We've had a break-in. A man with a gun entered and threatened—" My Bristol. Mine. "—the woman who lives here."

"Was the weapon fired?"

"No, I got to him first."

"Any injuries?"

"Yes. I beat the hell out of him."

"Is the intruder still conscious, sir?"

I glance at the crumpled mess on the kitchen floor. "No. But he's breathing."

"Does anyone else in the home have any injuries?"

The children here are going to have nightmares

about me for the rest of their lives. My teeth won't stop chattering. Sinclair is going to give me hell for punching a guy out when I have a concussion.

I'm a monster. It's not safe here. Hurry up.

"No. We just need somebody to take this guy away."

"Officers and paramedics are on their way. Should be a few minutes at most. I'm going to stay on the line with you until they arrive."

My throat closes up. Yeah, would you? Just stay on the line. That would be great. "Mm-hmm."

Bristol's got her arms around her siblings. A tear slips down her cheek. This is the last time I can let her look at me like this. It's the last time I can let her see me.

I'm not letting any more monsters get to her.

She'll be safe from all of us. Especially me.

Chapter Twenty-Seven
Bristol

NONE OF IT feels real.

Not the fresh apartment living room with the wide, cushy couch. Not both the twins curled up next to me on a Friday morning. Not the high-def TV playing a movie with the volume on low.

We've been out here all night, cuddling.

They didn't want to sleep alone in their bedroom, so I let them watch TV until they passed out. Not the best parenting move, probably, but they've had enough turbulence in their lives lately. I wanted them to know we had each other, the three of us, no matter what else happens.

Both of them woke up early. Brushed teeth. Picked a new movie.

I'm the only one watching. They're both asleep again.

I get it.

BLACKMAIL

Yesterday was a hard day.

The fight happened fast, but everything else took most of the evening. Police came to the apartment. Paramedics. Two of the cops took Will outside for a statement. I sat at the kitchen table with the twins and we repeated what happened. The cop was a kind, patient woman, but it still hurt to see the twins recount everything, to feel the fear vibrating through their small bodies.

Cops took the gunman away, handcuffed to a stretcher, still breathing.

Then the private security team showed up.

Six guys in the hallway. One of them swept the apartment to make sure there was nobody else hiding under the bed or in the closets. They were all clear.

Will never came back inside.

I saw him last at the opposite end of the hall, giving orders to a seventh guard. *Settle the debt with whoever is owed,* he was saying. *Get the word out that if anybody comes back here, there'll be hell to pay.*

He must have felt me watching, because he glanced over. There were five men between the two of us.

Will took a step back anyway. More distance.

He probably just needs some time.

He paid off the debt. He left an entire security team to guard the apartment. There's a car to take the twins to school and another one to take me wherever I need to go.

That must mean he's with me. That we're together.

But even a man as strong as Will Leblanc needs time to collect himself.

Mia stirs on the couch. On my other side, Ben stretches.

"Hungry?"

"Yes," they both say at the same time, then laugh. It's a tired, scared laugh.

They need time to collect themselves, too.

I'm standing in front of the fridge when my phone rings.

Shit. The temp agency.

Today is supposed to be my last day at Summit, but I haven't called in. No call, no show. That's a big deal in the world of temp agencies. I could be fired. I push the button to accept the call.

"This is Bristol. I'm so sorry I didn't call in. There was a situation last night, and—"

"Not a problem, Ms. Anderson. I'm calling to let you know that you're finished with the Summit assignment."

There's a lonely thump in my heart. "Oh, but—I still have one more day left on that contract. I thought I could go back on Monday and finish it. Or maybe I could work tomorrow. I know it's a Saturday, but—"

"There's no need." The lady on the phone is calm and kind. "A representative from Summit communicated to us that you've undergone some personal hardship. As a result, we're putting you on paid leave. You can let us know when you're ready for your next assignment."

"What?"

"Take as long as you need."

The temp agency doesn't have a paid leave policy. *As long as you need?* That's Will.

My eyes sting. The hollow of my throat aches.

The offer breaks my heart to pieces.

He's paying me to go away and leave him alone. He's making sure I never have to go back to the Summit offices again. If I'd been running a con, this would be a victory. All the debt has been wiped out and I have money to set up for the next thing. If I was like my father, I'd be dancing right now.

Except I'm not a con artist.

And I love Will Leblanc.

Or maybe I don't. Maybe I just care about him. I got curious, and I let myself care, and…

He doesn't want me back.

"Ms. Anderson?"

My chest feels tight. "Thank you so much for calling."

"Let us know if you need anything. Feel better soon."

Do I need anything? I need Will to hold me through the night.

I need him to tell me the sex wasn't just about blackmail. It wasn't just about fucking. It meant he cared about me, as crazy as that sounds. Even though he just paid me to go away.

I was essentially an overpriced escort for him. Too expensive. Too inexperienced. A bad deal.

A man like Will Leblanc didn't become successful by making bad deals.

You deserve somebody better, sweetheart. I'm not that guy. I'm a monster. You don't want me. I promise.

Is that what he really thinks about himself? Is that why he's staying away from me?

I have to find out. Because it's not going to end like this. Without even a conversation? With Will afraid to touch me? No. I have to find out if there's a chance he cares about me, too.

I stride to the front door of the apartment, pull it open, and stick my head into the hall. There are six guards wearing suits and earpieces outside, probably armed to the teeth, though I can't see any weapons.

"Carrie?"

One of the two women on the team today moves quickly down the hall and meets me at the door. "What can I do for you, Ms. Anderson?"

"I need to run an errand in the city. Could you wait inside with the twins?"

Mia and Ben have both tiptoed into the kitchen behind me. "Where are you going?" asks Mia.

"I'll be right back. I just need to talk to my boss

about something."

"Of course, Ms. Anderson." Carrie steps inside.

"Eggo waffles," I tell the twins. "As many as you want. I'll be back in an hour. I'm taking my phone."

Phone. Purse. Nothing else. Except for a boatload of courage. That's how much it takes to face Will after he basically fired me. *You're beautiful and sweet and delicate. I'm going to break you.* That's what he said to me, battered and bruised. Does he really think he'll hurt me?

An ache in my chest says it's too late. He's already hurt me. I'm already broken.

Another agent walks me out to a waiting car.

I give the driver the address for Summit.

It's a different story riding in a plush SUV. There's nobody else to stare at me or jostle me or catcall me while I keep it together.

Sidewalk. Main lobby. Elevator. The agent gazes professionally into space while we ride up.

The doors open, and I step out into chaos.

Absolute chaos.

People with boxes fill the lobby, waiting for the elevator. They cross back and forth, calling to one another. Even the receptionist is on her feet. She flips through files in her filing cabinet, loading them into one box. Supplies go into another. The quiet, beautiful lobby has transformed into a packing frenzy.

Her eyebrows go up as I approach the desk. "Ms.

Anderson."

"I need to speak to Mr. Leblanc. There might have been some confusion about my being out today, so—"

"He's not in." The receptionist gives me an apologetic smile. "We're spending the day packing up, but there's nothing on his schedule. He's already on site at our new offices."

My own smile is frozen in place. "No meetings?"

"No. He signed the paperwork for the merger with Hughes. It's all said and done." A little laugh. "So that was quick. Anyway, he said he'd be unavailable. Probably settling in over there. We're packing up fast. Supposed to vacate these premises by midnight."

"Wow." I don't know what to say. I don't know what to think. The solution that comes to mind is to sprint past the reception desk and through the office. Get to his desk at any cost.

But he's not there. He's already gone.

"It's not too bad," she says, conspiratorially. Because I'm like her. An assistant. The help. Not one of the fancy executives. "We're getting paid double time to finish up. And no one's getting laid off."

There's an awkward silence while we both register that I was, essentially, laid off. Not because of this merger with Hughes Financial Services, but because Will is tired of me.

It was temporary, and now it's over. He couldn't be

any clearer. Paid leave. Out of the office.

The twins are waiting for me back at the apartment. We need to start making plans. If Will's walking out of my life, his people will be leaving soon, too.

I force the smile back onto my face. "Okay. Thank you. Good luck with everything."

"You too, Bristol." I take two numb, faltering steps away from her desk. "Oh! Wait."

A call from Will. A message. Anything.

The receptionist holds up a small cardboard box. "These are your things, right? One of the interns got them from your desk. I was going to mail it to you, but this is perfect."

"Yes," I agree. "It's perfect."

I take the box.

There's a pencil holder inside that technically belongs to Summit. A tube of chapstick. A dish of tropical Jolly Ranchers. And my plastic palm tree. It looks sad sitting there in the tiny pile of cheap drug store items.

I follow the agent back into the elevator and outside to the SUV. I have two people to take me home, but that's not reality, is it? This isn't furniture I picked out and paid for. This isn't real life for me. It's imaginary, just like the idea that Will might care about me. The reality is that I'm left with a cheap miniature replica of my dream, alone as I was when I came to Summit for the first time.

On that day I dreamed about visiting a beach in the Bahamas, but that won't happen. Not ever. My dream expanded to include Will Leblanc. It wasn't only me that I imagined on that warm sand, coated with salt and sunshine. It was me and Will—and even the twins. It was a family.

It wasn't reality.

He might as well be on that beach in the Bahamas, because he's out of my reach.

Forever.

✧ ✧ ✧

Thank you for reading BLACKMAIL! Find out what happens to Bristol without Will to protect her in the next book. The stakes rise even higher in EXTORTION...

Will Leblanc takes risks in his private equity firm and in the underground boxing ring, but nowhere else. Definitely not in love. Which is why he had to walk away.

Except Bristol Anderson needs his help. More than that, he wants to protect her.

But no one can protect her from him. He has a dark side. A violent side. She's an unbearable temptation. He's barely holding back.

What happens when the monster inside him gets loose?

Will's brother Emerson has a book, too! You can read DARK REIGN now...

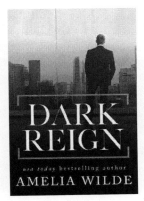

Wealthy. Reclusive. Dangerous. Emerson Leblanc doesn't enter society much. He only ventures out in pursuit of new art for his collection. It starts with a haunting painting. Then he meets the artist...

She'll be the perfect addition

to his collection.

> "An exquisite portrait of obsession that grabs you by the throat and doesn't let go."
>
> – #1 NYT bestselling author Laurelin Paige

Remember the man Will meets at the restaurant?

Finn Hughes knows about secrets. His family is as wealthy as the Rockefellers. And as powerful as the Kennedys. He runs the billion-dollar corporation. No one knows that he has a ticking time clock on his ability to lead.

Eva Morelli is the oldest daughter. The responsible one. The caring one. The one who doesn't have time for her own interests.

Especially not her interest in the charismatic, mysterious Finn Hughes.

A fake relationship is the answer to both their problems.

But there's no chance for them. No hope for a woman who's had her heart broken. And no future for a man whose fate was decided long ago.

The warring Morelli and Constantine families have enough bad blood to fill an ocean, and their brand new stories will be told by your favorite dangerous romance authors. See what books are available now and sign up to get notified about new releases here...
www.dangerouspress.com

About Midnight Dynasty

The warring Morelli and Constantine families have enough bad blood to fill an ocean, and their brand new stories will be told by your favorite dangerous romance authors.

The beauty will sacrifice everything to the beast…

Haley Constantine will do anything to protect her father. Even trade her body for his life. The college student must spend thirty days with the ruthless billionaire. He'll make her earn her freedom in degrading ways, but in the end he needs her to set him free.

READ SECRET BEAST >

> "Secret Beast is the dark and delicious Beauty and The Beast re-telling I've been craving. Leo Morelli is an EPIC hero and I could stay in his world forever!"
>
> – M. O'Keefe, USA Today bestselling author

In a single moment, she becomes my obsession…

Elaine Constantine will be mine. And her destruction is only my beginning.

I've known all my life that the Constantines deserved to be wiped from the face of the earth, only a smoking crater left where their mansion once stood. That's my plan until I see her, the woman in gold with the sinful curves and the blonde curls.

READ HEARTLESS >

My will to dominate her runs as deep as the hate I have for her last name.

No matter how beautifully she bends beneath my hands, I'll leave her shattered, a broken toy for her cruel family.

Tiernan arrives all dressed in black. Diamond cufflinks. A watch on his tanned wrist that cost more than we would ever see in a lifetime of work. He carries a single red rose…

It turns out he is my new guardian.

READ DANGEROUS TEMPTATION >

"Dark, decadent and provocative, Dangerous Temptation is one of my absolute favorite reads in 2021. Tiernan and Bianca set my Kindle on fire! Giana has weaved an exquisite story, I can't wait for the next. READ THIS!!!"

– RuNyx, bestselling author of Gothikana

SIGN UP FOR THE NEWSLETTER
www.dangerouspress.com

JOIN THE FACEBOOK GROUP HERE
www.dangerouspress.com/facebook

FOLLOW US ON INSTAGRAM
www.instagram.com/dangerouspress

About the Author

Amelia Wilde is a USA TODAY bestselling author of steamy contemporary romance and loves it a little too much. She lives in Michigan with her husband and daughters. She spends most of her time typing furiously on an iPad and appreciating the natural splendor of her home state from where she likes it best: inside.

For more books by Amelia Wilde, visit her online at www.awilderomance.com.

Copyright

This is a work of fiction. Any resemblance to actual persons, living or dead, business establishments, events or locales is entirely coincidental. All rights reserved. Except for use in a review, the reproduction or use of this work in any part is forbidden without the express written permission of the author.

BLACKMAIL © 2022 by Amelia Wilde
Print Edition

Cover design: Damonza
Formatting: BB eBooks